The Date

Single Wide Female in Love
Book 1

By

Lillianna Blake

ISBN: 069251726X
ISBN-13: 978-0692517260

DEDICATION

To all the single women out there.
Never give up on love. ☺

TABLE OF CONTENTS

CHAPTER 1..7

CHAPTER 2.. 13

CHAPTER 3.. 19

CHAPTER 4.. 25

CHAPTER 5.. 31

CHAPTER 6.. 35

CHAPTER 7.. 41

CHAPTER 8.. 47

CHAPTER 9.. 53

CHAPTER 10 57

CHAPTER 11 61

CHAPTER 12 65

CHAPTER 13 71

CHAPTER 14 77

CHAPTER 15 83

CHAPTER 16 89

CHAPTER 17 95

CHAPTER 18 101

CHAPTER 19 107

CHAPTER 20 113

CHAPTER 21 119

CHAPTER 22 125

CHAPTER 23 131

CHAPTER 24 137

CHAPTER 25 143

CHAPTER 26 147

CHAPTER 27 153

CHAPTER 28 159

CHAPTER 29 165

CHAPTER 30 171

CHAPTER 31 175

CHAPTER 32 181

CHAPTER 1

"I've never been so in love."

"Looking into your eyes is like looking into the heavens."

"Oh, you're so sweet!"

"It's true!"

I chugged down the remainder of my wine. After eavesdropping on the couple at the next table, I felt even more uncomfortable sitting alone at my own. Max had invited me to dinner, but he was late.

To distract myself, I reached into my purse and pulled out a folded piece of paper. I glanced around to be sure no one was paying attention before unfolding it— although it really wasn't a huge secret as I'd been blogging about my list for months now.

My life had been turned upside down—and not in a bad way—the moment I'd decided to create a bucket list. It was a list of things I longed to experience but hadn't because of my weight. It inspired me to remain focused on my weight loss as I checked off each item.

I needed that inspiration again. As I read over the list, my eyes lingered on a smudged spot where an item was erased.

Kiss Max

I remembered writing it. I also remembered erasing it. Max and I were best friends. That was all we would ever be, no matter how madly in love I was with him. I needed to find a way to accept that. So I'd erased the item from my list.

As I sat in the crowded restaurant filled with people who all appeared to be in love, I made another decision. It was my bucket list, and if I wanted Max to be on it, then he would be. I pulled a pencil out of my purse and scribbled the item back on the list, smiling as I did so.

Kiss Max

I doodled a little set of kissy lips beside the note. Maybe Max would never love me the way I loved him, but that didn't mean we couldn't share one single amazing mind-blowing over-the-moon heart-melting kiss!

"Hi, beautiful."

His touch on my shoulder made me jump out of my chair. I grabbed the paper so fast that I knocked over my wine glass. Luckily, it was already empty. Max set the glass upright and laughed as he sat down across from me. "Sorry. I didn't mean to startle you, Sammy."

"It's okay. I guess I was just lost in my thoughts."

"What were you thinking about?" He gazed across the table at me.

I ducked my head to hide the heat in my cheeks.

"Oh, just what to order for dessert."

I eyed the dessert cart as it rolled past. I had to wonder who ever thought up the idea of the cart. How was it deemed a good idea to pile a cart up with every delicious dessert in the restaurant and then roll it tauntingly past the patrons? I found it hard to believe that there was a single person in the restaurant who did not want to devour the entire thing. I knew for certain that I did.

"Sammy?"

I forced my eyes away from the decadent desserts and settled them on something just as tempting. Max. He looked even more handsome than usual in a suit jacket and tie.

"Hm?"

"I asked how the book was coming?"

"Oh, no. We don't talk about that at the table." I picked up my glass of water and took a sip to mask an anxious grimace. Ever since I'd decided to become a writer full-time, my progress was asked about by everyone.

Max laughed. "Okay, sorry. I just thought maybe

that's why you're so quiet tonight."

"Am I quiet?"

"Yes. If there's one thing I can always count on with you, it's a good conversation. But you seem a little distracted."

"I'm sorry."

"Don't be. I just want in on what's going on in that creative mind of yours."

For just a moment I was distracted by creative thoughts about Max. Max without his shirt on, Max with those perfect lips headed for mine, Max...

"No!"

I winced as I realized from Max's stunned expression that I'd spoken out loud.

"Okay. You don't have to tell me." He furrowed a brow and looked down at his food.

I took a breath and tried to focus. My new goal in life was not to want the things I couldn't have. Max was something I could never have. Maybe a single kiss, but certainly not a lifetime.

"What I meant was that you don't really want to know." I did my best to laugh off my behavior.

"Sure I do." Max met my eyes. "Out with it, Sammy."

I smiled. It warmed my heart to have a friend like Max who knew just how to get the truth out of me.

"Alright, but don't say I didn't warn you."

"I can handle it."

"I've decided that I'm going to fall in love."

"Oh?" Max stared at me. His lips twitched at the corners.

I thought he was going to laugh. Instead he picked up his drink.

"Yes. It's been long enough. It's time that I experience true love." I watched as he set his glass back down without taking a sip.

"Do you have anyone in mind? Taking things to the next level with Greg?"

I shook my head. I'd really tried to make things work with Greg, the guy that I'd been seeing for awhile, but at the end of the day, I couldn't kid myself. The spark just wasn't there, and I wanted the spark. I turned my thoughts back to Max's question. "No, things aren't going to work out with Greg, but—well, there is one person."

"Ah, that guy—what's his name? Green or fuchsia or something?" He raised an eyebrow.

"Blue." I laughed. Max had a sparkle in his eyes as he teased me. "Actually, his name is Matt."

"Matt." Max shook his head. "So how do you propose to make yourself fall in love with Matt?"

"I don't have to make myself." My lips curved into a dreamy smile. "That part is easy. I just have to make him fall in love with me."

Max reached across the table and took my hand. "Anyone would fall in love with you, Sammy."

Anyone but you.

For a moment I wondered if I'd actually made the

statement out loud.

CHAPTER 2

Max let go of my hand and sat back in his chair.

"Thanks, Max. But I don't think it's that simple. I mean, I don't want to wait anymore. Either he falls in love with me, or I find someone else to fall in love with. I'm ready now. I want that next stage in my life. I write about romance, but how can I write about true love if I've never experienced it?"

"I think it's great that you want to be in love. But it's not something that can be forced, is it? It has to be with the right person."

"I agree. How can I ever meet the right person if I'm pinning my hopes on the wrong one?"

I glanced over at a couple seated not far from us. They looked just like Max and me. Both engaged in conversation. Both too occupied to eat their food. Both smiling and laughing. But the other couple wore wedding rings. I loved Max. I valued him as my best friend and the most important person in my life. But I wanted more than a good conversation. I wanted a conversation that didn't end.

"Give him a chance."

I looked back at Max and realized I had missed most of what he said.

"Who?"

"Blue."

"I'm going to. But I'm not going to wait forever. Either he's ready, or he's not." I heard the determination in my own voice. It was nice to be so set on a decision. In the past I'd let the desires of others dictate my choices. Now I was ready to make my own decisions based on my needs.

"And if he's not?"

"Then he's not the right person. I am not going to be strung along." I picked at the last of my food. "If there's one thing I've learned over the past few months it's that if I don't make something happen it's not going to happen. As long as I sit here waiting for love, love isn't going to show up. I need to get out there and find it. If it's not with Blue, then it's not."

"I'm surprised by that. If you feel so strongly for this person, why won't you be patient?"

Max's tone was a little cross. I looked up at him.

"How patient can I be?" I raised an eyebrow. "He's had plenty of time to make a move—to make it clear to me that he cares for me the way I care for him. Is this some kind of male pride thing—to see how long a woman will twirl in the wind waiting?"

"That's not fair." Max grinned. "Though it is a funny image. I just mean, maybe he has a good reason. Maybe he's shy."

"Fine, I get that. I've been shy. I've wanted to hide from the world and never be seen for fear of being judged. But, if he can't see that I accept him no matter what, then we don't have the kind of connection that I thought we did."

"So you'd give up on him?"

"Whose side are you on?" I laughed.

"Sorry. I guess I just haven't heard you talk about someone like this before. So tell me more about this guy. What is it that you like so much about him?" Max turned his attention to his food.

I considered the question. I hadn't made a list of all of the things I liked about Blue. I just knew that I did.

"He gets me." I shrugged. "He's so supportive and understanding. He likes the way that I think and I like the way that he thinks."

"But you have no idea what he looks like. He could be anyone."

"Sure. But does it really matter how someone looks? I could be sitting across from the most beautiful man I've ever laid eyes on, but that doesn't mean he's the one for me." I did my best to hide the truth in my words. "I think that attraction doesn't matter as much as connection. Have you ever considered that you could connect with someone that you weren't necessarily attracted to?"

"Of course." He took a bite of his food.

It seemed to me that it was a well-planned bite to avoid saying more.

"Well, with Blue it honestly won't matter to me what he looks like. As long as he is the person that I've gotten to know over the past few months, I will be overjoyed to meet him."

"You can't know that until you meet him."

"Okay, fine, but I'm going to meet him, so that won't be an issue anymore."

Max set down his fork and looked across the table at me. "I just want you to be happy, Sammy."

"I'm working on it." I laughed. "I am happy. I've made so many changes in my life. My body is changing, but that's not even the best part. My self-confidence is growing. I'm getting to know who I truly am. I thought I could go on just like this and be satisfied. But the more I grow, the more certain I am that I want to share my life with one special person. I just want the chance to experience that true passion. Sitting and waiting on the sidelines hasn't worked so far. It's time for me to go out there and grab it."

Max grinned. "I guess that's one way to make sure you get it."

"Well, to tell you the truth, there are no guarantees. I might end up alone in the end. But at least I will know that I tried."

"There's one thing I can promise you." Max looked

into my eyes.

"What's that?"

"You're never going to be alone."

My mind filled with thoughts of Max and me walking down the beach at sunset, Max and me cooing over baby clothes, Max and me traveling to new places together.

No! I cleared my throat. "You're right, Max. No, I'll never be alone." I smiled at him.

LILLIANNA BLAKE

CHAPTER 3

Max dropped me off at my apartment after dinner. I didn't even look in his direction. Just when I thought my feelings for Max were purely friendship he had to go and be amazing. My determination not to lust for him faded in the warmth of his eyes. So I didn't look.

I walked up to my door, stepped inside, and closed it behind me. I might have imagined Max chasing after me and begging me for a kiss. But only for a moment.

I shook my head to clear my thoughts. That just made me dizzy and still longing for a kiss.

Since I couldn't seem to get romance off my mind, I decided to put it into my writing.

In my new book, romance was brewing. I sat down in front of the computer and began fiddling with what I'd already written. I focused on how I felt when I thought about Blue, Max, or even another potential mate. I did my best to integrate my emotions into the character. In many ways she reflected my own personality. It was cathartic to slip into her world and explore without consequences in my own world. I settled into the story and began typing away.

An hour slipped by. I had to get up and stretch. As I walked around my apartment I thought about love. I really thought about it. Love as a reality, not just an idea. I always thought of love as something in the distance, something in my future. I never really considered what it would be like to have it in my own life.

"Wow, here I am trying to write about love, but I have no idea what it is."

I thought about watching some romance movies or even reading some romance. But that was all fiction. It was all imaginary. The plot line was set before the actors took the stage. It was predictable and took no one by surprise. I needed to see real love. Not what made blockbuster hits, but the kind of everyday love that made marriages span decades.

It was still fairly early in the evening, so I decided to go for a walk. Maybe if I saw love in action, I would get a better idea of what it actually was. Plus, I would get my exercise in for the day.

As I walked, I people-watched. I noticed a young couple cuddled up at the bus stop. Their arms were intertwined. Their eyes were glued on one another. It was silly, sappy love that made me smile. But would it last? Anyone could be fascinating for the first few weeks. What then?

I caught sight of a couple in their later years struggling to get through the door of a shop. The woman had a cane to deal with and the man was carrying all of the bags. As he tried to get out the door, she grabbed for his arm to keep her balance. He dropped a bag and leaned down to get it. She stumbled forward. He was there to catch her.

"Be careful, Frederick!"

"I'm sorry. Maybe if we didn't have to buy all of these things I wouldn't have dropped the bag."

"Oh, I'm sorry if eating is a problem."

"Eating isn't the problem, but we are only two people—why all of the groceries?"

"Really, Frederick, not this again."

"I mean it. I'd be happy with peanut butter sandwiches."

"I'm sure your sugar levels would be perfect after that." She rolled her eyes.

I thought for a moment that I was about to witness the crumbling of romance. A moment later though, Frederick had her elbow gently grasped in his palm.

"Are you okay? Did you get hurt?"

"No, I'm fine. Here, I'm sure I can take a bag or two."

"Not a chance, my love. I've got it."

As the two walked down the sidewalk, I smiled just as much as I had when I'd noticed the young couple. Maybe that was the point. Maybe love wasn't just one thing, or one way. Maybe it changed and grew just as much as we all did. If that was the case, it could look different to everyone. It was probably experienced differently by everyone.

I wasn't going to find an example of the love I would have, because it didn't exist yet. That was both empowering and a little scary. What if I never had it? What if there was no version of love for me? The thought hurt.

I was sure of one thing, I didn't want to be alone for the rest of my life. If it meant that I really had to get out of my comfort zone and put myself out there, then that was what I would have to do. I was ready to change my life, but was life ready to change for me?

As I walked back toward my apartment, I noticed a man standing outside one of the shops. He stuffed his hands into his pockets and gazed at the passing traffic. He didn't seem to be going anywhere or waiting for anyone. He was just standing there. The sight made me a little uneasy. Didn't he have things to do? How could he just waste time standing and staring?

As I drew closer to him I noticed that he was humming a melody. It sounded sweet. Enchanted, I slowed and then stopped beside him. It took him a moment to even realize that I was there.

"Oh, excuse me, am I in your way?"

"No, I'm sorry. I was just listening to that melody you're humming. It's lovely."

"Oh yes." He laughed. "I forget that I'm doing that sometimes. It's a special tune for me."

"Can I ask why?" I didn't question strangers often but

his demeanor left me intrigued.

"It was the song at my wedding." He rocked back on his heels and looked back at the traffic. "I like to hum it when I'm remembering."

"Remembering?"

"Oh, you know—the better times. Sometimes I just take a few minutes out of my day and remember. It makes hard times a lot easier."

I didn't need to ask why times were so much harder. There was no wedding ring on his finger. Somehow the marriage he once valued had ended. Yet he could still use the memory of it as comfort to get through the day.

"Thanks for sharing with me."

"No problem." He returned to his memories.

I continued down the sidewalk. That was a kind of love too—the kind that lasted forever, even if one partner wasn't there to share in it anymore. I didn't want to just date someone, I wanted them to want to remember me for the rest of their lives. I wanted to be the good thing in their hard times. I wanted them to be the same for me.

It would be tough to find, I was sure, but I was up for the challenge.

LILLIANNA BLAKE

CHAPTER 4

When I returned to my apartment I sat down at my computer again. Instead of trying to write more, I opened my e-mail. The last note I received from Blue was another vague promise that we would get together. That wasn't enough for me. Not anymore. I sent him a reply.

Blue, we need to talk.

I stared at the screen. I waited for what in my mind was about two minutes and in reality was more like ten seconds. Then I typed another message.

Hello?
Are you there?

I normally have a policy that I will not send repeated e-mails or texts. I might have had a brief encounter with text addiction that landed me under my covers at three in the morning staring at the screen of my phone waiting for a text. However, today I didn't mind sending multiple e-mails. I wanted his attention. I demanded it.

I was about to hunt down a meme about respect and what it means to me, when Blue sent back an e-mail.

What's wrong?

I scrunched up my nose. What's wrong?

I want to talk.

His response came back right away.

We are talking.

I rolled my eyes and tried not to take my frustration out on the keyboard.

I want to talk on the phone. How is it that we are planning to meet and I still don't even have your phone number? I want to hear your voice. I want to know that you are actually there.

I realized that quite possibly I wasn't making a lot of sense. I stared at the screen.

Several minutes went by before Blue finally e-mailed me back.

I'd been patient, as I expected that he was writing a very lengthy response that would account for the delay.

Instead I read a very short note.

I have a sore throat. Not up for talking. I'm sorry.

That was it. That was the final straw. I did not e-mail him back.

Yet again, he'd refused to give me any of his contact information. I felt foolish for asking in the first place. I was so upset that I was ready to shut down my e-mail account.

Then the guilt began to pile on top of me. Maybe he really wasn't feeling well. Maybe I was being cruel to him when he needed compassion. That's when it hit me. All of the canceled dates, all of the avoided phone calls, were changing me. They were turning me into someone I didn't want to be anymore.

I walked back over to my computer and sat down again. There was another e-mail from Blue.

Samantha,

Are you upset? I thought you wanted to talk? Just tell me what's going on. We can figure it out.

Blue

I began to type without even thinking about what to say first.

Dear Matthew,

I'm confused. You tell me that you want to meet me, that you have feelings for me and that I should trust you. Then you show me that you want nothing to do with me by ignoring my requests for phone calls, failing to show up for our dates, and making vague promises.

I think I've made it clear that I want you to be part of my life—my real life, not just my virtual life.

I can no longer be patient. I have waited long enough. If you truly want to be with me, then you will find a way to meet me. This is the last time I'm going to ask. I value you, Blue, and what we have together, but I have to value myself too.

You know how hard I've worked at making progress. I have no interest in going backward. I want to go forward. If you want to go forward with me, then we need to take the next step and meet.

Samantha

I stared at the e-mail. Should I send it? Had I said too much? Was I overreacting?

I decided to delete it. But when I went to click the delete button, I clicked send instead. An instant later the e-mail had gone out. My stomach twisted.

What would he think when he read it? Would he say that I was asking for too much? Would he just ignore it and never contact me again?

I stood up and began to pace back and forth. The

anxiety that rattled my mind made me want to hunt down whoever invented e-mail and smack them. Why, oh why did I send that e-mail?

To my surprise I received an e-mail back within minutes. I sat down and braced myself for what it might say.

Samantha,

It breaks my heart that you think I don't value you, but I understand why you do. I'm sorry that I've been so neglectful. There is really no excuse for it. You tell me when and where. I will be there. No matter what.

Blue

It was short but to the point. I hoped that he meant it.

Now the pressure was on. I had to pick the place and time. If I gave him the benefit of the doubt in believing that he was sick, he would need a few days to recover. I decided to plan it for the following Saturday. It would give him plenty of time to feel better.

Blue,
Saturday night. La Villa. 7.

Samantha

I sent the e-mail before I could change my mind.
Then I waited for the excuse.

Samantha,

I will be there. I won't disappoint you again.

Blue

CHAPTER 5

After I read Blue's response, I felt my whole body buzzing with excitement. Maybe it would finally happen. Maybe!

I jumped up out of my chair and began dancing around the living room. It didn't matter to me that no music played. I didn't need to hear it to dance to my own rhythm. As I was spinning and dancing I thought about what my life would be like with Blue in it. Maybe we would spend every minute we could together. Maybe we would curl up inside each other's arms and never pull apart. My heart still raced as I gave up on dancing and plopped down on the couch. I flipped on the television to help settle my mind.

The movie appeared to be a romance. I smiled to myself and began to watch. Then I realized that the scene was about a woman being stood up.

"Ugh!" I flipped the channel.

"Yes, I thought I was in love once, but I was wrong. I've been alone ever since." The elderly woman grinned into the camera. "Guess love isn't for everyone."

"Seriously?" I changed the channel again.

"This just in, Hollywood's sweethearts are breaking up in a messy way. Everyone has something to say about it. With his reputation, she should have known better!"

"That's it!" I turned off the television and tossed the remote down on the couch. I decided it would be better to try to go to sleep. At least then I wouldn't be assaulted by stories of broken hearts.

I curled up in bed and closed my eyes. I wanted to feel excited about the date with Blue. Instead, my mind filled with all of the reasons why he might not show up. Who was I to demand that anyone meet me? All of my insecurities crept through the subtle cracks in the self-esteem I'd built up.

I tried to push them away with positive thoughts.

I am valuable. I am beautiful. I know that I am worthy of love. But all of those thoughts didn't seem to do anything to combat the worry in my heart. If no one in my life had ever fallen in love with me before, why did I think it would be any different with Blue?

I flipped over in bed, as if changing sides might change my point of view. In the darkness of my room a tickle of loneliness threatened to burst my confident bubble. I thought of the young couple, so passionate and addicted to one another. I thought of the older couple, accustomed to each other's quirks and still in love. I thought of the man alone on the corner, humming his wedding song.

Yes, there were many different kinds of love. Would I ever have my own?

I opened my eyes to the subtle song of a bird outside my window.

Okay, it was not that subtle, and it might have been a thump of the bird flying into my window.

I sat up and was struck by a wave of dread. It socked me right in the gut and threatened to knock me back down into bed. I should have been excited that I'd finally set a date with Blue. Instead, my mind filled with all of the reasons why he wouldn't show. The most prominent reason: he didn't want to.

No amount of reassurance shifted the inner dialogue that seized my mind.

I forced myself to roll out of bed. As I trudged into the kitchen, the weight of the world threatened to crush me. Instead of the buzz of happiness that I had experienced in the past, I braced myself for inevitable disappointment.

I was sure that if I continued to hope, Blue would disappoint me again.

As I obsessed about these thoughts, I battled the urge to eat to silence my feelings. I wanted to feel better, and a treat used to be a way to get me to that happy place. After all of the progress I'd made with my weight loss, I didn't want to throw it away due to feeling inadequate.

"No way. I've got to get control of this." I marched into my bedroom. The floor-length mirror on my wall displayed my reflection. "Sammy, you've worked hard. You're not going to throw it away over a man's opinion."

I wanted to be inspired by my pep talk. I waited for that billow of pride that would remind me of how important my weight-loss journey was. Instead, dread washed over me yet again. It troubled me that Blue had such an influence on how I felt about myself.

Maybe that was the problem. Maybe I needed to remind myself that there were other options.

As the idea formed in my mind, a smidgeon of excitement perked up within me. I prepared a healthy breakfast and then sat down at my computer. I opened up the website of the online dating service I'd used a few months before.

Sure, Blue was the man that I wanted. But he wasn't the only man out there. I could distract myself with potential matches and build my self-confidence at the same time.

CHAPTER 6

Since it had been so long, I needed to update my profile on the dating site. I was eager to change some things—like my body type and my career. But other questions were still a stumbling block for me. One in particular was difficult.

"What is your ideal mate?" I read the question out loud. That didn't make it any easier to answer.

I didn't really have any specifics when it came to looks. But I had a lot of requirements when it came to personality. I began typing in the best description that I could. I mentioned that I valued a positive attitude, supportive nature, and creativity. I added a few other things and then moved on in the profile.

When it came time to select physical characteristics, I realized I didn't want to be picky. Just like I hoped a potential date would be interested in me and not how I looked, I wanted to do the same for him. I marked all categories and only limited the age range a little. I was ready to truly branch out and see who was out there looking to fall in love too.

As soon as I made my profile public again, my body jolted with enthusiasm. This was it. I was on the hunt. I felt a slight twinge of guilt for publicizing my profile with dinner plans in my future, but I no longer felt that sense of dread. If Blue came through then I would forget all about MatchMe. If he didn't show up, I would at least have something to distract me from the heartbreak.

As I surfed through the profile pictures, I was impressed. The faces I saw smiling at me didn't seem like strangers. To me, they were on the same journey—in search of love.

With this warmth filling my heart, I clicked on one of the profiles. As I read through the description that warmth started to disappear. The man I'd chosen had very particular interests that had nothing to do with personality. The graphic requests he made left me with a sick feeling in my stomach. I shut down his profile and sat back in my chair for a moment. I wasn't sure if I wanted to risk clicking on another profile.

Was that what the online dating scene was now? All I wanted was the chance to get to know someone, but maybe that wasn't the way it was done anymore.

I clicked on the profile of another man. He looked handsome and his description sounded much better than the last. I clicked on the box that showed I was interested.

As I began looking through a few more profiles, I did find a dud or two, but there were also some quality guys to choose from. Of course all I saw was what they wanted me to see on their profile. The next step was making actual contact.

That step didn't take long though. I started getting notifications of messages right away. As I read through them my hopes were dashed. There were quite a few requests for hook-ups. I had zero interest in that kind of connection. Then I came across a sweet message that asked for an opportunity to get to know me. I sent a note back that invited him to message back and forth with me. The more messages I received the more potential dates I accepted.

I could have spent all morning sitting in front of the computer browsing through profiles and responding to messages. Luckily, I had a breakfast date with Max to distract me from doing just that. I did, however, download the dating app onto my phone before leaving.

It was amazing to see how many men out there had an interest in meeting me. Of course I knew that some of them were less than genuine and some might even be dangerous, but with so many responses I was sure there had to be a handful of good guys in there.

As I walked into the restaurant, Max stood up from his booth and waved to me. I walked over and gave him a quick hug. When that familiar inkling of desire sparked, I reminded myself that I had plenty of other men to spark with.

"How are you this morning?" Max sat down across

from me.

"Good. Excited."

"About your date with Blue?" Max smiled. He pushed a menu across the table to me.

I picked it up and began looking through it.

"Sure. That should be fun." I didn't look away from the menu.

"So, that's not what you're excited about?"

"Not just that."

"Then what?" Max pulled the top of the menu down slightly to look at me. "Do you have a surprise for me?"

"Maybe." I laughed.

I decided on scrambled eggs. Once I had given my order to the waitress I turned back to Max. I opened my mouth to speak but before I could, my phone began chiming. I glanced at it to see that I had received several notes from men. I ignored them and put my phone back down.

"I think things are about to move in a positive direction for me."

"Oh. Well, that's good." Max nodded.

I noticed him staring at my phone. It chimed a few more times. I picked it up and looked at the screen. I was about to ignore it but the picture of one of the men drew my attention. One little tap and I was browsing his profile.

"Sammy?"

"Oh, sorry." I put my phone down. "That was so

rude."

"It's okay." Max laughed. "But our food is here." He gestured to the waitress who waited politely beside the table.

"I'm so sorry." I blushed and sat back so that she could set my plate in front of me. I couldn't remember the last time I had checked my phone in a restaurant.

CHAPTER 7

Once the waitress walked away, Max looked across the table at me.

"So tell me about this positive change."

"Sure. It's just that I need to get out more, you know?" I paused as my phone chimed again. I couldn't resist. I picked it up and was about to look when Max snagged the phone right out of my hand.

"What are you hiding from me?" He grinned.

"Max!" I tried to snatch the phone back.

"I'm just taking a look." He caught a glimpse of the screen of the phone. "Seriously?"

He handed the phone back to me with a funny look in his eyes. "You're on MatchMe?"

"So?" I frowned. I didn't mind Max snatching my phone. We didn't have any real secrets. But I didn't like the way he was looking at me.

"So, I thought you were with Blue?"

"Matt."

"Right, Matt."

"I'm not with anyone. How could I be with someone

I've never met?" I shook my head. "We have a date planned, but I doubt that he's actually going to show. I'm not going to let myself get disappointed when he doesn't. I decided I wanted to see what was out there. If I'm going to find love, I have to go looking for it."

"But MatchMe isn't the place." Max shook his head. "I've heard so many horror stories about that. Look, you have no idea who you are agreeing to meet, then you show up and you could be in real danger."

"I have no idea who Blue is either."

"That's different. Haven't you been talking to him for a while? I mean you must know him pretty well by now."

"It's not different." I frowned. "The Blue I think I know wouldn't keep canceling on me. Anyway, I'm not going to meet any of these guys. I'm just seeing what's out there. If Blue shows for our date, then he shows and we'll go from there. If not, I'm not waiting any more. I told him that too. There are other men in the world that want to be with me, that will make time for me, that will show up when they say they will."

"Wow." Max stared at me. "I didn't know that you were that serious about finding love."

"Shouldn't I be?" I set my phone down. "Like my mother tells me all the time, I'm not getting any younger."

"Oh, that's crazy." Max laughed. "You've got plenty of time, Sammy."

"So what if I do, Max? What if I don't want to wait that long?" I sighed. My patience was running thin. "I just want to be loved, Max. What's so wrong with that?"

Max's smile faded. "I understand that, Sammy."

"Do you?" I frowned. "I know that dating comes so easy for you. But I don't want to just date, I want to put my whole heart out there."

"I think that's a beautiful idea. I just don't want to see you get hurt." Max pointed to my cell phone. "If one of those men can make you happy, that's great. They're just going to have to go through me."

I grinned. "I'm sure."

"I mean it." Max offered a stern look. "I retain veto power."

"Oh really? I didn't know we had that. I would have used it on that blonde that had the chihuahua!"

"Sparkles? Hey, the dog was pretty adorable." Max laughed.

"He should have been named Sprinkles for what he did to your carpet."

"Oh, I'd almost forgotten about that." Max shook his head. "Thanks for the reminder."

"We'll see. Who's to say that I'll even meet anyone?"

The wind left my sails a bit as I glanced around the restaurant—lots of beautiful couples, lots of wedding rings and engagement rings.

"I'm sure you will. I just think you should try it out the old-fashioned way. Get to know somebody local. Meet people."

I laughed. "And how am I going to do that, Max?

You're the only one who ever takes me out to dinner."

"I'm not such bad company, am I?"

I smiled and did my best not to let him know that he was terrible company. Not because he wasn't witty, or intelligent, or attentive, but because when I looked at him I thought of things I shouldn't.

"Not at all."

"Well, just promise me you'll be careful."

"I promise."

After breakfast I took a stroll around the park. I made it a point each day not only to exercise, but to be around people. It helped me to get more comfortable with being seen. Too much of the past few years was spent trying to be invisible.

The park was dotted with dog walkers, moms with toddlers, and people feeding the squirrels. There wasn't much to draw my attention. I could hear my phone chiming in my purse. I couldn't resist any longer.

I cut my walk short and sat down on a bench. Then I began looking through the notifications from men interested in meeting me. A few that I connected with sent me messages. I read over them. One was flirty. I sent a playful quip back. He immediately responded with a kissy-face emoticon.

"Kissing already?" I laughed.

As I sent a message back my hopes lifted. No, this guy wasn't Blue. He never would be. But he was someone who thought I was worth his time and attention. So far that put him in a better category than Blue.

I sent a few more flirty texts back and forth with him, then he said he had to go but would love to talk later in the day. I agreed. It felt good to look forward to a conversation with someone new.

Blue knew just about everything there was to know about me. He'd been reading my blog ever since I started it. He knew about my struggles as I checked off items on my bucket list. In some ways that was a wonderful thing. In other ways, maybe it wasn't. If he didn't know so much about me, he might make more of an effort to actually meet me.

CHAPTER 8

I left the park with mixed feelings about what to expect next.

When I arrived home, I headed straight for my computer. For the first time in months I did not check my e-mail right away. Instead, I logged into MatchMe to tweak my profile. Once I was done with that, I checked my e-mail.

When I saw an e-mail from Blue, I expected he intended to cancel the date. I clicked on the e-mail and gritted my teeth.

Samantha,

I'm really looking forward to our date. I hope that you are too. I know that I've been more than a little elusive. I'm sorry if that's made you feel insecure about me. You astound me every day with your insights and determination. I only wish that I could be half as brave as you. You may not realize how much you inspire me, but you do.

I have a lot to tell you when we get together. I know you've been waiting for some answers to some questions, and I plan to give you those answers. Thank you for being so patient with me while I sort through some things. I can't wait for us to finally take the next step.

Blue

The first time I read the e-mail I was flooded with warmth and desire. To hear Blue's opinion of me was a huge compliment. However, I could not overlook the fact that it was still very vague. A part of me wondered if he had somehow seen my profile on MatchMe. The thought worried me and at the same time I hoped it was true. Maybe he would see that I was serious and manage to make it to our date this time.

I read over the e-mail again. At least it wasn't a cancellation. But it was a reminder that Blue kept things from me. What were his secrets? Was he a spy? I laughed a little at the idea. There were so many things that I could imagine. But I didn't want to imagine any more. I wanted to know the truth. Once and for all I wanted to be able to push forward with our relationship. As much as I wanted to believe that he wanted that too, I couldn't bring myself to. I just didn't want to be disappointed again.

"Try to keep your heart open, Sammy." I sighed. "Maybe, just maybe, this time it will happen."

I rested my hand against my chest just over my heart. Part of my journey had been learning to love myself again; the other part had been learning to accept love from others. I still struggled with both.

With so much emotion racing through me, I was ready to do some writing. I spent most of my afternoon doing just that. I did not respond to Blue's e-mail. I wanted him to sweat it out a bit. I knew that playing games was not like me, but I also wanted to make a point.

After I'd written a quite a bit, I took a break to prepare lunch. As I danced through the kitchen putting together my meal, my phone chimed. I nearly dropped my salad in my rush to get to it. I hoped it was a message from the man on MatchMe. Instead it was an alert about an e-mail from Blue.

Did you get my last e-mail?

I smiled a little. "Aha, so now you're the one demanding attention." I sent a quick response back.

Yes, I did.

I nodded. That should be vague enough. His response was swift.

Are you upset with me?

The question melted my heart. In my mind, Blue didn't care. That was why he broke all of our dates. But what if that wasn't the case? What if he did care and I was toying with his emotions?

I could never be upset with you. Thank you for the e-mail. It meant a lot to me. I am looking forward to our date too.

I sent the e-mail and then put my phone down. I knew if I continued to e-mail back and forth with him I would end up asking him questions that he wasn't ready to answer. I would do my best to be patient.

I tried to focus on my work, but every time I slipped into the role of my main character to write a chapter or two, I felt such a deep longing for that kind of love in my real life that it bled into my words. I had to delete several passages, because I was determined that the heroine of my story would never be that desperate. Instead of being able to move forward as I'd hoped, I found myself stuck in the same paragraph of text.

As my date with Blue drew closer, my insecurities were spiking all over the place. So Blue had agreed to the date, but only because I'd threatened him. Was it fair of me to force him into something that he obviously wasn't ready for? I felt like an emotional mess. I wasn't going forward, I was going backward. I needed to get my head back in the right place again.

One of the best ways I'd found to ground myself was yoga. It was my go-to to get my body limber and get my mind relaxed.

I particularly enjoyed the five breaths I took in each pose. It sounded silly to me at first when the teacher instructed me not to forget to breathe. Who could forget to breathe? Then I found myself holding my breath, not just when I was doing yoga, but throughout my day. I would hold my breath without even realizing it when I was tense or stressed. I started to pay attention to my breathing process rather than neglecting it.

I needed to come up for air.

CHAPTER 9

When I arrived at the yoga class I was relieved to see some familiar faces. I'd let a few of my good habits fall by the wayside after shifting careers. It had been a few weeks since I'd been to the class. My body showed it, when I joined in. It was stiff and unyielding. It took a good warmup to get it to begin to cooperate.

As we were moving through the positions I felt my body heating up. Even though there wasn't a lot of cardio in this particular class, it was always a workout for me. The toning had done wonders for my midsection.

As I lifted my leg back and up into the air, I released a heavy breath. It was nice to remember that my body was capable of more than I realized. My mind drifted as I held my position. I tried to direct myself toward peaceful thoughts, but instead I thought of all of the connections on MatchMe waiting for me to look at.

My leg began to throb. I opened my eyes to see that everyone else was in lotus position. I had missed a few transitions. As I hurried to catch up, I lost my balance and ended up in the belly-flop position—which was not an actual position.

"Samantha, are you okay?" The woman beside me looked like she was trying to hide a smile.

Most of the other students in my class were familiar with my clumsy tendencies.

"I think so." I grinned at her.

"Don't worry. We all get a little lost in our heads sometimes. It's hard to keep the balance."

At first I thought she meant my physical balance, but as the teacher walked us through a few minutes of meditation, I realized that what I'd lost was not my physical balance as much as it was my mental balance. When I decided to throw myself headlong into finding love, I'd forgotten most of what I'd learned. Yes, I could hunt for love. But falling in love wasn't who I was. It wasn't all of me.

"Thanks for the reminder." I smiled at her.

"The universe speaks to you if you listen." She winked at me. "Of course sometimes it says get the heck out of the way. That's what it's been telling me lately."

"Really?" I laughed. "How do you know?"

"I made plans. I ironed out each step I would need to take in order to succeed. Then I took the first step. I got slapped with the flu so hard that I was out of commission for a week. I recovered and took the next step. My family got spun around by a crisis and I had to focus all of my energy there. Once that was settled, I took the next step. I literally walked into a brick wall because I was so busy texting someone about the business on my phone."

"Wow, that sounds like something I would do. In fact I've probably done it a few times."

"Well, I was pretty frustrated. I felt like everything was against me succeeding. I was angry and stressed. I was snapping at my family, isolating myself from my friends—I even stopped meditating. I was totally out of balance and didn't even know it."

"Sounds familiar." I grinned. "What did you do?"

"It just hit me one day that if it was this hard, I didn't want it. I was losing myself in my desire to make it happen. I let go of the idea and I refocused on my inner life. A few days later the business partner I had planned to work with admitted that she didn't want to do it either and had planned to pull out. A day or so after that, a brand new opportunity presented itself that worked much better for me. The entire time, I had wasted so much energy trying to force something to happen that was never going to happen." She laughed as she shook her head. "I look back on it now and feel pretty embarrassed about my behavior."

"But you couldn't have known." I frowned.

"Maybe not, but if I had stayed in balance and listened to my instincts I might have saved myself a lot of grief." She picked up her yoga mat. "I guess the point I'm trying to make is that if you're trying to force something, it's probably not the path to take."

I thought about her words after I left the class. Life

appeared to have a simple formula. Make a plan. Go for it and achieve it. But I'd had many experiences that proved otherwise. Maybe she was right about not forcing things.

Was that what I was doing with Blue?

CHAPTER 10

The next day I decided to check in on my friend Anisa at Fluff and Stuff. She'd been the manager for some time and I was sure that she was getting the hang of it. The truth was that I missed the place and wanted to stop in. I was hoping that it would help get me back into balance. Even though I enjoyed being a writer, there was something therapeutic about the smell of laundry soap and the whir of the washing machines.

When I opened the door to Fluff and Stuff, I was greeted by that familiar scent. A very strong scent. And very loud whirring. I opened my eyes to see suds floating all over the floor. Anisa brandished a mop as she battled the flow of water. Three of the washing machines trembled so hard that they moved out of their position against the wall.

"Anisa, what happened?"

"Samantha! You're like a laundromat superhero! How did you know I was in trouble?"

I laughed and shook my head. "I didn't, but it sure

looks like you could use a hand."

"I can't get to the machines to shut them off."

"I've got it!" I jumped up on top of a dryer and then made my way across a few more machines to the offending washers. I felt particularly limber after my yoga class. I also did feel a bit like a laundromat superhero. I was much more than just a woman waiting to fall in love. I could conquer great sloshing beasts!

I turned off the washing machines, though that didn't stop the flow of water immediately. I stood on top of one of the machines as if it were a mountain I'd climbed.

"Anisa, you are saved!"

Anisa laughed as she looked at me. "My hero!"

I jumped down from the washing machine and nearly slid across the floor. As my arms cycled through the air frantically in an attempt to regain my balance I laughed out loud at the situation.

"Some hero!"

Anisa came to my rescue and grabbed my arm to steady me. Once I had my footing, I grabbed a mop to help her.

"Oh, Samantha, you don't have to do that. It's my mess."

"It's no problem. I could use a little distraction." As we worked on getting the water and suds out of the laundromat she filled me in on her recent adventures.

"So, I'm pretty sure we're going to get married!" She grinned as she looked at me.

"Wow! Congratulations, Anisa!" I hugged her tight.

"Thanks. I didn't think I would take the plunge, but it's amazing how my mind changed after I met him."

I smiled fondly at the thought. That knowledge that you wanted to spend the rest of your life with someone was something I had felt before. I still felt it. First with Max, then with Blue. I could understand why with Max—he was my rock and my biggest fan.

But Blue—I hadn't even met him. Maybe I needed to be a little more realistic about my feelings for him.

"So what have you been up to?" Anisa took the mop from me and put it back in the closet.

I flipped on the switch for the fans so that the floor would dry out.

"Writing. Well, to be honest, I've been trying to find love." I braced myself for her reaction. Anisa was the type to tell it like it was without sugarcoating anything.

"How's that going?" She raised an eyebrow.

"It's a bit more difficult than I expected. I guess I was hoping for rainbows and fairies." I grinned.

"I know. Wouldn't it be nice if the man of your dreams glowed gold or something when you saw him?" Anisa laughed. "You could just say—hey, you—you right there, you're mine!"

I laughed too. "That would be perfect!"

"Too bad it doesn't work that way." Anisa shook her head. "But you'll figure it out in time, Samantha. You have to give yourself room to be loved."

"What do you mean by that?" I was curious.

"I mean, you can't always be looking for it. If you're always looking for it, you might look right past it. You have to invite it. Be ready and open to it. Then let it find you." She shrugged. "At least that's some of the stuff my mother used to tell me. But then she ended up getting married three times, so who knows?" She laughed. "All I know for sure is that I wasn't looking."

"Interesting." I nodded. "So maybe I should stop looking? But it's so much fun to look. There are so many men out there and they are all an opportunity, right?"

"You can look at it that way. But the thing is, if you believe like I think you do, there's really only one. That one is going to show up whether you're looking or not."

"I'm not sure I believe that any more. But thanks for the advice."

"No problem. Thanks for saving me from the flood."

"Just make sure that you clean out the hoses. Sometimes they get backed up."

"I will." Anisa smiled. "And don't worry, Samantha. It'll happen. When it does, you won't even remember what it was like to be waiting for it."

As I left the laundromat I hoped that Anisa was right.

CHAPTER 11

The next day I tried to focus on myself instead of finding love. I focused on being ready for it, inviting it in, and being open to all of the possibilities. But as the hours ticked down, I found it harder to keep my head above water. All I could think about was Blue.

The thought of him occupied my mind throughout my day and well into the night. I found that it was nearly impossible for me to sleep. I was either fantasizing about Blue or terrified that things would turn out to be a big flop.

I had to wonder if this was why he'd been avoiding our first meeting. Was he as worried about it as I was? I finally got some decent sleep the night before our date. I had reached a point of exhaustion that I could not fight against. My stomach ached on an almost constant basis.

"If this is what love feels like, maybe it's not so great."

I crawled out of bed and tried to get my bearings. I didn't want to panic. I didn't want to stress. I wanted to rely on all of the lessons I'd learned over the past few months. I could meditate to calm my anxiety. I could use the power of positive thought to transform the way I thought about the date. I could dance, stretch, leap, and twist in an attempt to keep my mind off the upcoming date.

However, nothing I could do would prevent me from thinking of Blue. I was more than excited to finally meet him. But I was also incredibly nervous. When we met would the chemistry still be there? Was most of our connection based on our both being so anonymous? Or was I trying to force something that just wasn't the right path?

"I guess I'll find out tonight."

I headed for my closet. I had an idea of what I wanted to wear, but of course I second-guessed it. I didn't want to look like I was trying too hard, but I also didn't want to miss out on what might be my one chance to truly wow him. Of all the firsts that couples had—the first kiss, the first dance, the first fight—Blue and I had a very unique first to share. Everyone had that first moment when they first saw one another, but I had the distinct luxury of planning for mine.

I decided to try on a few different outfits to see which one felt right to me. I laid out a simple dress, a skirt and blouse, and a pair of cute jeans with my favorite top. The restaurant we were going to wasn't fancy. It was more like a dressed-up diner.

As I tried on the different outfits, I noticed the changes in my body. I'd worked hard to see those changes. I wanted to feel confident, but I kept looking at my reflection through his eyes. Would he mind that my thighs were so full? Would he notice the way my hips jutted out?

I decided against the dress because the sleeves were too short and my arms were still flabby. I decided against the jeans because they were just a little tight around the waist. Darn that dessert cart.

I was left with the skirt and blouse. As I hung the outfit back up for later that night, I frowned. Despite all of the work I'd done on my self-confidence, I still didn't see beauty when I looked in the mirror.

"Maybe this was a bad idea." I tugged on some jeans, and a t-shirt that was baggy enough to hide what I thought were my flaws. As I walked into the kitchen, my body seemed bulkier and heavier. By the time I reached the kitchen I didn't see a point to choosing a healthy breakfast. It didn't matter—not if I still didn't look the way I wanted to—did it? I opened the fridge and began searching for something sinful. As I was searching, my phone began to chirp with a new message.

I gave up on my hunt, as I kept mostly healthy foods in the house, and checked the phone. There was a message from Ben, a man on MatchMe that I had sent a few messages back and forth with.

Are you available tonight? I can't wait to meet you.

I frowned as I studied the message. Ben had been pushing for a meeting, but I didn't actually want to meet anyone. I just needed the ego boost and something to fall back on if things didn't work out with Blue. But the more I learned about Ben, the more curious I became about him. I didn't like stringing him along.

Not tonight. I will let you know tomorrow if we can get together. Thank you for the invite.

I smiled a little when he sent a happy face back. It reminded me that there were men out there that found me attractive. With all of the media focused on perfect bodies in tiny swimsuits, it was easy to think that my body type was repulsive. But it wasn't.

Just like I was attracted to many different kinds of men, men were attracted to different body types too. If Blue couldn't accept me for how I looked, then I had a good feeling that Ben would.

I decided that I would wear what I liked best, without considering how anyone else would view it—my favorite top and my cute tight jeans. That was who I was—casual, fun, and lighthearted. That was how I wanted to look.

CHAPTER 12

About an hour before the date, I got dressed. I applied a little make-up. I fiddled with my hair. Then the pacing began.

All afternoon my focus was on positive thoughts and deep breathing to prevent anxiety.

But all of that went out the window as the time started ticking down. With each minute that passed my heart beat faster. I was excited, but I was also terrified. What if he didn't show? What if he blew me off yet again?

How would I handle that? I picked up my phone and called Max. After several rings he answered.

"Hey, Sammy."

"Max, I need a favor from you."

"Anything."

"I need you to be on call for me—just in case things don't go well with Blue."

"Oh yeah, that's tonight, huh? Are you sure you're up for it?"

"I'm trying to be."

"Well, if he doesn't show, it's his loss."

I sighed and closed my eyes. "I know what you mean by that, Max, but no, it won't be his loss. It'll be mine. It will be a huge loss. Because I really, really want him to be there. I just need to know that I can call you if he doesn't come."

"You can always call me."

I wondered if he was with someone. He was keeping his answers short. Was he tired of me blathering on about Blue and my anxiety about the date? Was he impatient with my neverending insecurities?

"Thanks-Max."

"Sammy. You know, no matter what, you're an amazing woman. He'd have to be nuts not to show up."

I smiled at his words. "You think so?"

"Of course I think so. Just call me."

"I will."

"Be careful."

"I will."

"Sammy."

"What?"

"You're beautiful. You could have any man in that restaurant. Just remember that."

I rolled my eyes. I did not believe that for a second. But I knew his intentions were good.

"Thanks for the pep talk. I really appreciate it."

"I've got to go." His voice wavered.

I wondered if he had a girl next to him. Was she

kissing his neck? Was she rubbing his knee? Was that why he had to rush off the phone? I started to get jealous, then I had to laugh at myself. Here I was about to go out on a date, and I was jealous of Max, being on one of his own. It would be good for both of us if I began dating someone. I was sure that Max could use a break.

After I hung up with Max I felt a little better. I was ready to meet Blue. I looked in the bathroom mirror for a final check of my make-up and hair.

"This is going to be the best night of your life, Samantha. There's no reason to worry. You are going to have a great time. This should be exciting."

I coached my own reflection. It felt good to say positive things, but it did not erase the twinge of deep fear that was still stabbing me in the gut.

I grabbed my purse and pulled on my favorite shoes. Then I headed out the door. A part of me wished I'd asked Blue to pick me up at the apartment. Then, at least, if he didn't show I wouldn't be in public. But I thought having our first conversation trapped in a vehicle together might be a little awkward.

Instead, I drove my car toward the restaurant. I turned up the radio to build up my excitement and to drown out my fear. With every mile that I got closer to Blue, my anticipation built. Earlier in the day I was so preoccupied about how I would look to Blue that I hadn't really considered how he might look to me.

What if he was much older than I expected? What if he was grotesque in some way? That would explain why he had avoided our date so much. I thought about the different issues he might have with his looks. I realized that I really didn't care what he looked like. He could have a third eye and I would still feel the same way about him.

When I parked the car in the busy diner parking lot, I glanced around at the other vehicles. I wondered which one might be his.

Then I reminded myself that I was a little early. Blue might not even be there yet. I braced myself for the possibility.

I stepped inside the diner behind a large group of people. With so many in front of me there was no way to even get the hostess's attention. I had to wait for them to be taken care of first. As I waited, I tried to peer past the glass barrier that separated the dining area from the entrance. I wanted to see if Blue was there yet. Then I realized how silly that was. Even if he were there, I was not likely to recognize him. Once the people in front of me were guided to their seats, the hostess returned. She smiled at me.

"Cute jeans."

"Thanks." I beamed back at her. Hearing a compliment from another woman was a special kind of confidence-builder. It was given freely, without expectations, and it meant that she truly admired my jeans. "Is anyone waiting for Samantha?"

"No, I'm sorry I don't have anyone waiting right now. Would you like me to get you a table?"

"Yes. I'm waiting for someone to arrive. Matthew."

"Okay, let me get you settled." She smiled and led me to a table in the center of the diner.

I noticed there were quite a few people seated around it.

"Do you have anything more private?" I smiled a little. "It's kind of a special night."

"Oh, sure. Let's see." She surveyed the dining room. "There's an empty spot by the bathroom. Is that a problem?"

"No, that's fine." I was relieved at the idea of being so close to a place to hide. If I said or did anything silly I could excuse myself easily to the restroom. She led me over to the table.

"Would you like a drink or would you like to wait for your date?"

I liked the sound of that. Date. Blue was my date. I tried not to giggle with excitement.

"I'll wait."

CHAPTER 13

Once she was gone, I glanced around at the other people around me. They were all couples. I was surprised that there wasn't a single family or a mother and daughter duo. It was quite clear that all of the people at the tables and booths around me were madly in love with one another. I liked the idea that there was so much love surrounding me. Maybe those good vibes would rub off on me and Blue.

While I waited, I began looking over the menu. I wanted to make a healthy choice, but I also didn't want to be stuck eating a salad while he was eating something amazing. There were a few options on the menu that would keep me in my calorie range.

I glanced up toward the door. A few people walked in. None of them seemed to fit my idea of Blue.

It was still early. I looked back at the menu. As I immersed myself in the various options available, I thought about all of the dinners I'd shared with Max. My comfort level with Max was so good that I didn't even think about what I ate in front of him. He never noticed or pointed out that I could have made a better choice. Our friendship was not like that. Max accepted me for who I was. How could I not fall in love with that?

Then Blue showed the same desire to love me just the way I was. I was lucky. I'd be even luckier if he would actually show up for our date.

I counted the tiles on the ceiling. I noticed some watermarks. I tapped my foot beneath the table. I tried to focus on my breathing.

I'll be there. I won't disappoint you again.

I chanted the words over and over in my mind. Stay calm, Sammy, he would have to be a terrible person not to show. Just relax. I took a deep breath and looked back at the menu. When I noticed that I had reread the same description for the third time, I put the menu down. My entire body was tense. I tried a meditation technique to ease the strain on my muscles.

Three, two, one, relax.

Three, two, one, breathe.

Three, two, one, where the heck was he?

I fiddled with the napkin on the table. It was a paper napkin made to look like a cloth napkin. I thought it was pretty interesting. It was stronger than most paper napkins. I was curious about how it was made stronger. Okay, maybe I was trying to distract myself from the fact that Blue still hadn't arrived.

There were bubbles of anxiety rolling around inside of me. I knew if I let one pop I was going to start freaking out. I didn't want to do that. I wanted to remain calm and not panic. I wanted to be the Samantha I'd been trying to become over the past few months.

Then it happened. The waitress began walking toward me. I did my best not to look at her. I hoped she would take the hint and not approach me.

"Ma'am, are you sure I can't get you anything while you wait?" The waitress smiled.

"No, thank you." I tried not to bite her head off. I really didn't want it pointed out to me that I had been sitting there long enough to draw the attention and sympathy of my waitress.

Blue was ten minutes late. Ten minutes could be traffic. It could be a wardrobe malfunction. It could be just about anything. I took a breath and focused on remaining in balance. He promised to come. He would be there. He would never hurt me like that. Even if he were a secret spy on a mission to save the world, he would make sure that he was there. He promised.

I did my best not to look at the door. I didn't want to look anxious and desperate when he saw me for the first time. The bubbles of anxiety had turned into an ache of dread. No matter how I tried to deny it, it was happening again.

Just when tears began to well in my eyes, a man walked toward me. He was older than I expected, but his features were ruggedly handsome. As he continued toward me I felt my excitement level increase. This was it.

This was the moment when I would meet the man who had helped me through some of my toughest moments. He paused beside my table and looked into my eyes.

"I'm so glad you're here!" I knew it wasn't the most romantic thing to say, but it was all I could think of.

He cleared his throat. "I'm sorry, this is a little awkward. It's just that my wife and I have been waiting for a table for a long time. It's our anniversary and we had our first date here. We'd really like to eat here, but we only have the babysitter for so long and there are no tables available. I saw that you've been sitting here alone for some time, and I figured you're getting ready to leave. So I wondered if maybe we could have your table?"

If he hadn't been so kind about it I probably would have doused him with my glass of water. I was feeling so many things at once—hot with embarrassment, tight with fury, and absolutely disappointed. Yet somehow through all of that I could recognize the sweetness of the man's request. He and his wife had the type of love that I longed for. It wasn't his fault that he'd found it and I hadn't.

"Sure. You can have it. I was just leaving."

I picked up my phone and my purse.

The waitress noticed me stand up. She nodded to me with sympathy as I walked away from the table. There was no bill to settle because I hadn't ordered anything. There was only the long walk of shame to the door of the restaurant. With each step my stomach twisted to the point that I thought I might get sick. I squeezed my eyes shut tight in an attempt not to cry.

As soon as I was outside I texted Max.

I need you.

It was a pathetic message, but it was the truth.

My entire body quivered in anticipation of falling apart. I tried to focus on getting to my car, but I couldn't think of driving. I wanted to hit something. I wanted to break something. Most of all I just wanted to cry.

"Why promise me that you will be here and then not show up?" I summoned my strength and did my best not to notice the people who were staring at me. I couldn't blame them, since I was pacing back and forth along a busy sidewalk talking to myself.

With forced steps I headed in the direction of my car. At least there I could hide away.

Once inside, I rolled down the windows. I still wasn't ready to drive. I hadn't heard back from Max. I imagined that he was occupied with some beautiful woman. Really, it wasn't fair of me to always demand his attention.

LILLIANNA BLAKE

CHAPTER 14

I tried to call Max. I knew it wasn't right, but I was scared of going home and bingeing. I needed to be around someone who actually thought I was worth showing up for. Of course he didn't answer. His phone rang and rang. I heard the ring tone right outside the car. When I turned to look, Max was standing beside the open window with a bouquet of flowers.

"I'm sorry. I got your text and I wanted to bring you something special." He gazed into my eyes with such warmth that the tears began to flow.

Max opened the door and opened his arms to me. I leaned out of the driver's seat to hug him. He held me so close that I thought for sure he would be exhausted by my weight and my sobs. Instead he continued to hold me. "I'm so sorry, Sammy, I'm so sorry." He kissed the top of my head. "You can't let this get to you. You're an amazing woman. You deserve so much, and this is not it." His voice shuddered.

I pulled back enough to look at him. The tears in his eyes shocked me. Did he really care so deeply for me that he couldn't stop his own tears?

"I'm sorry, Max, I'm a mess."

He offered me a tissue. "You're not a mess. This is a mess." He sighed.

I wiped at my eyes with the tissue and tried to calm down. "I just really thought he'd be here." My voice cracked as more tears threatened.

"He should have been."

"But he wasn't."

"I'm sorry. I'm so sorry." He hugged me again.

"Do you think you could drive me home?" I sniffled. "I just don't want to drive like this."

"No." Max shook his head.

I was hit in the gut again. Was Max rejecting me too?

"I'm not going to let you go home and hide away. You look gorgeous." He swept his gaze over the outfit I'd chosen. "You planned for a night out and you're going to have one."

"Oh, Max, no." I frowned. "I'm really not up for it."

"I'm really not giving you a choice." He held his hand out to me.

When I looked from the flawless skin of his palm to the heat in his eyes my emotions collided once more. There he was, the perfect man. The man I had been in love with for years. He was always there for me, no matter what. He supported me and comforted me. He was right there in front of me, making me love him even more. But I could never have him. Max was just too beautiful, just too perfect, to ever be with someone like me. I lowered my eyes and shook my head.

"I don't want to, Max. I think I should just go home."

"Nope, not having it." He grabbed my hand and tugged me out of the car. "We're going to go for a walk."

My body crackled with electricity in reaction to his touch.

"Like this?" I shook my head. "I look ridiculous."

"You look beautiful." He tugged again.

I stood up. There was no point in arguing. I wouldn't trade anything for time with Max. I took a deep breath of the air around us.

"I just don't think it's ever going to happen, Max. I don't think the universe is going to align to deliver me the man of my dreams."

"Do they come in the mail now?" He tilted his head to the side. "I didn't realize."

"Ha ha—you're not going to cheer me up."

"Oh, I don't intend to."

We started walking toward a path that led into a small garden.

"Good. Because I have a right to be grumpy and I'm going to be."

"I wouldn't expect anything else." He winked at me.

I scowled at him. "How can you take this so lightly? He broke my heart!"

"Really?" Max gave my hand a little squeeze. "Because I think your heart is much stronger than that."

"Nope, don't think so."

"Hm." He glanced up at the tree we were walking past. "Look at that." He pointed at a bird's nest on one of the limbs. It had tiny little babies in it.

"Aw! Look how cute they are!" I cooed and gazed up at them.

"See, I told you. I don't have to cheer you up. You find a reason to be happy pretty easily."

"Oh, that's your plan, huh?"

"I mean it. You're much stronger than you give yourself credit for Sam. I'm sorry this happened—you have no idea how sorry I am. But don't tell me that your heart is broken, because your heart is the strongest I've ever known."

"You don't have to say things like that." I paused and turned to look right at him. "I'm sorry I'm always drawing you into my drama."

"You're not. I'm here because there's nowhere else I want to be."

I smiled. "I just wish that Blue felt that way."

"I'm sure he does."

"Right, because he's here."

"Some things are hard to understand."

I looked at him with disbelief. "Why are you defending him?"

"I'm not." He released my hand. I felt the absence of his touch as if it was oxygen leaving my lungs. "I'm sorry. You're right."

"Max, why are you so good to me?" I searched his eyes.

"Because I love you, Sammy." He smiled at me.

"I love you too, Max." I opened my arms for a hug. When he wrapped me up, I felt content. Even though I wanted so much to fall in love, I was grateful to have such an amazing friendship with Max.

CHAPTER 15

Max pulled away and I caught sight of his eyes. It was accidental, but I saw it. I saw the passion there. I stared at him as he turned away from me.

"Max?"

"Hm?"

"Are you seeing anyone right now?"

"Why?" He smiled a little.

"I just feel like we're always talking about me and my dating life. I haven't heard much about yours."

"Oh you know, dates here and there." He shrugged.

"No one you're interested in?"

He licked his lips and glanced at me. Then he looked away again. "Not really."

"Why do you think that is? I mean there can't be something wrong with all of these women."

Max shifted from one foot to the other. "What's with the interrogation?"

"Forgive me for being curious." I smiled sweetly at him.

"Curiosity can lead to some dangerous things." He

turned back to face me. I thought he would have a big smile on his face. Instead he looked a little nervous. "Are you willing to take that risk?" He met my eyes with such a serious expression that I couldn't resist giggling.

"You're too much, Max."

He pursed his lips and shoved his hands into his pockets. "You didn't answer the question."

"There's nothing dangerous about you."

He abruptly wrapped his arm around my waist and pulled me so close that the breath left my body. It was such a sudden shift in position that I couldn't process it. Max's body was pressed against mine from hip to chest and I thought for sure that he had to feel my heart, as hard as it was pounding. He met my eyes with a wicked smirk on his lips.

"Are you sure about that?"

All of the desire that I so carefully locked away to maintain our friendship came spilling out into every nerve of my body. I was bathed in my need for him. With his lips so close to mine the temptation to throw caution to the wind and just kiss him was so intense that I shivered. His eyes widened in reaction to me wriggling in his grasp. The smirk faded into a satisfied smile.

"See?" He winked at me.

"Max."

"Sammy." He leaned a little closer to me.

Good lord, was he trying to kill me? I flushed and tried to even out my breathing. I didn't want to make a fool of myself. I started to lift my chin to get the perfect angle for a kiss. Then I looked into his eyes. Max's eyes. Not Blue's. Not some random guy I was on a date with. The eyes that belonged to my best friend who had dropped everything to come to my aid. A man who had made it clear to me in the past that he was not interested in me in that particular way. Was it fair for me to try to steal a kiss when it wasn't mine to take? Those soft lips belonged to another woman, one he hadn't met yet, one who would spend the rest of her life kissing them.

"I should go."

I untangled myself from his grasp. For just a second his muscles tensed as if he might hold on to me. Then his arm fell away.

"I'll take you home."

"No, it's okay. You're right. I'm stronger than I think. I'll be fine. How could I not be, with you by my side?"

Max studied me for a moment. The way his eyes tightened and his jaw rippled made me think that he was about to speak, but instead he only nodded.

"Alright. I'm always here if you need me. Always."

I believed him, but in that moment I needed to be as far away from him as possible. If I looked into his eyes a second longer, I was going to take what I wanted even if it meant losing our friendship.

As I walked away from Max, I felt in many ways as if I was walking away from Blue too. There was no question that I was in love with both men, but that didn't matter. I couldn't make either of them love me back—not the way that I wanted them to.

It was time for me to let love come to me as Anisa had advised. I couldn't force it, I had to invite it. The first step was letting go of the love I had tried to possess for myself.

After I put the flowers Max gave me in water I poured a very tall glass of wine. I hadn't had dinner, so I knew I was going to get tipsy. But that was okay. I didn't have anywhere to go or anyone to please. I had every intention of maintaining a positive attitude.

I sat down at my computer and turned it on. Right away I saw an e-mail from Blue. Maybe he had sent it before dinner. Maybe there was an excuse. Maybe it was a good one. But I didn't want to read it.

I deleted the e-mail. I felt strong and I was done waiting.

I logged in to MatchMe and began perusing my connections. Right away Ben sent me a note.

Are we on for that date?

I took a sip of my wine and stared at his photograph smiling at me. He was a handsome bigger guy. I liked the way his smile reached his eyes in the picture. More importantly, he had gone out of his way to make himself available to me.

Absolutely. You name the time and place and I'll be there.

That started the ball rolling. It continued until my glass of wine was empty. By the time I turned off the computer I had a date lined up for just about every night the next week. It made me feel good in a way to know that I was wanted.

But as I gave in to the rumble in my stomach and put some dinner together for myself, I was still disappointed that I'd missed out on my chance to meet Blue. It occurred to me that I would always wonder about him.

CHAPTER 16

My first date with Ben brought back a little of my excitement in finding love. Being stood up by Blue still smarted, but I thought the best way to get over it was to dive right into the dating scene.

Ben had been eager to meet, so we set up a date for the next night. I liked that he was so willing to drop everything to see me. The restaurant he chose was a midpoint between our two homes. I'd never eaten there before and I looked forward to trying it out. It was being promoted as a whole food restaurant with lots of fresh choices.

I noticed Ben as soon as I parked. He stood near the front door. His fingers drummed awkwardly against the slope of his thigh. I was not instantly attracted to Ben. I wanted to be, but there was something about his mild demeanor that made him a little hard to pay attention to.

I ignored that. Attraction could grow as we got to know one another.

I walked up to him with a wide smile. "Ben?"

"Samantha!" He stared at me. "I didn't think it was

possible but you're prettier than your picture."

I could feel my face getting hot at the compliment. He was being kind, and to be honest, I needed to hear it after what had happened with Blue.

"Thank you. I'm so glad that we have the chance to get together."

"Our table is waiting." He opened the door. "Unless you'd rather eat somewhere else? We can go wherever you want."

"No, this is perfect, thanks. I've been curious about this place."

"Great." He held the door open for me.

I mentally made a note that he was quite polite.

As we sat down at our table, he kept looking up at me. I smiled each time he did. I felt the need to put him at ease. Once we'd ordered our drinks, I decided to take the lead in the conversation. I knew what it was like to feel so nervous.

"So Ben, what do you like to do for fun?"

"I collect stamps. I know that's boring. Who even does that any more? But I was raised by my grandfather, and it was our way of bonding. So I still do it—as a way to honor him."

"I think that's very sweet. There's nothing wrong with collecting stamps. It's interesting to think of all the places that they've been."

"Yes, exactly!" Ben laughed. "I can't believe you get it. Yes, it's really not even about the stamp itself for me, it's more about where it's come from. My sister used to joke that I just needed to find a woman who liked to collect postcards—that we'd be a perfect match."

"She has a point." I grinned. "I'd love to see your collection some time."

"Great." He tapped the table lightly. "That's great. So, Samantha, what do you do for fun?"

My mind filled with all of the activities I'd engaged in over the past few months. The list was too long. I didn't want him to think that I was flighty.

"Well, as a writer, of course I really enjoy writing. But I also have gotten to know—I guess you could say my spiritual side."

"Oh? That sounds interesting. Contemplating your navel?" He grinned.

"Not exactly." I laughed. "But I have been trying to connect with myself—you know, who I really am."

"How's that going?"

We paused as we ordered our food, then Ben looked back at me. "Have you learned anything surprising about yourself?"

I smiled at the question. I hadn't really thought about it before. "I think I'm much more daring than I ever knew. I have an adventurous side. I've been trained not to take risks, but I think at my core, I really enjoy it."

"Wow! That would surprise me, because I don't take any risks. Okay, actually the only risk I've taken is joining the dating site, and I only did that because my sister made me. I like things to be a certain way—expected, so that I can relax and just enjoy life."

"That makes sense. You really have the chance to savor your experiences if they are predictable."

"Predictable." He cringed. "That's probably a bad thing."

"I don't think so." I shook my head. "Knowing what you want, achieving it, and living it—that's all pretty amazing in my book."

"You're really easy to talk to, Samantha."

"Thanks."

As we shared our meal, I learned a little bit more about Ben. He wasn't lying when he said he hadn't taken any risks in life, but I admired that about him. I began to think he would never be able to handle my "live in the moment" lifestyle. By the time we'd finished our lunch, I wasn't so sure that we'd be seeing one another again.

"Thanks, Ben. I had a nice time." I smiled politely at him.

"I hope we can do it again soon. What do you think?" Ben's hands trembled a little as he waited for my answer.

"Sure, I'd really like that."

Why not?

"When?"

"How about Tuesday? If you're not busy?"

"No, not busy at all. To be honest, Samantha, you're the only woman I've connected with from the site."

"Oh, I didn't realize." I decided against telling him

that I had gone on a matching binge. "But I'm glad you're free. We could do dinner. How does that sound?"

"Perfect." He nodded. "Wow. I didn't think you'd say yes."

I laughed. "Why not?"

"I don't know. Most women don't say yes."

"Well, I'm glad they didn't. That gives me the chance to say yes now."

Ben and I shared a quick hug after we left the restaurant.

It felt strange to me to even think of kissing him. As much as I hated to admit it, Ben was right. I probably shouldn't have said yes. I just didn't feel any chemistry between us. But I wasn't going to let that ruin our chance. Chemistry could come later.

CHAPTER 17

As I listed all of the positive aspects of meeting Ben in my head, I sent a text to Max.

Great date. Looking forward to seeing him again.

I smiled at being able to text that—no drama, no raw emotion, just contentment.

Max didn't need to know that initially I might need to force myself not to see Ben as a brother figure rather than a love interest. I didn't know what it was about him that made me want to be his buddy and not his girlfriend, but I planned to overcome that.

At home I headed straight for the computer. I wanted to add some depth to one of the scenes I'd been working on where my main character first encounters her love interest. I'd been stuck on how to get that connection going, but now I had a better idea of how it felt to interact at that first meeting.

On a whim I checked my e-mail first. My heart sank when I saw another e-mail from Blue. I'd not written him back since deleting his first two e-mails. This time I would read it. I wanted to know that he was okay.

After clicking the e-mail open, I immediately regretted it.

Samantha,

I'll do anything.
You name it. I'll do it. Please.
I know that I failed you again. I can't even explain why. There are no excuses for what I did. I feel awful about it, but that doesn't even matter. What matters is that I hurt you when I promised that I never would. I can't begin to apologize. I know that I don't even deserve the opportunity.

I can't just say goodbye, Samantha. I need to see you. When we meet, you'll understand. At least, I hope you will. That can only happen if you give me just one more chance. I know I'm out of chances, but I also know how kind and forgiving you are. I'm asking for you to have mercy on me, because if I have to spend the rest of my life never having told you the truth, it will be pure torture. I know that's selfish of me, but I think you need this too. I know you care for me the way I care for you. I know that you feel this connection between us.

Please, give me one more chance.

Blue

The impact of the e-mail was not what I expected. I

thought I might be angry, or even sad. Instead, I felt relief. Relief that Blue still cared. I knew I shouldn't be swayed so easily, but it warmed my heart to think that he hadn't given up on me—that he wouldn't.

That, however, did not mean that I was willing to forgive him. My fingers ached to type a message back, but I refused to do it.

I wanted to take some time to think things through. I wanted to go on my dates and discover how I felt around other men. Blue had made me wait; now I was going to do the same to him.

To distract myself from thinking about Blue, I started chatting back and forth with Spence, whom I had a date with the next day. He was very responsive.

Can we talk on the phone?

I wasn't sure how to answer that. I figured it couldn't hurt to give him my number if we planned on meeting the next day. I sent him the number in response.

A minute later my phone began to ring. My heart jumped but I didn't have time to be nervous.

"Hello?"

"Samantha?"

"Yes, is this Spence?"

"Yes. Wow, what a beautiful voice."

"Oh, thanks." I felt my face getting warm.

We weren't even in the same room and he was already getting under my skin. I'd never thought about how my voice sounded.

"About tomorrow—I had some ideas. What do you think about food carts?"

"Uh—some of the food can be great."

"So you wouldn't care if we ate at one?"

"As long as it's one you've been to before." I cringed at the idea of eating at some side-of-the-road roach coach. The food carts I'd eaten at in the past were all highly recommended.

"It's my favorite place."

"Okay, I'm up for trying it." I smiled. The last thing I wanted to be was picky. Sure, it wasn't what I'd expected, but that didn't mean that it couldn't be great.

"You don't care that it's not a sit-down place?"

"Not at all. If that's what you like, let's give it a shot."

It was an unusual way to have a first date but I was determined to be as open to new ideas as I could be. Spence sounded like a passionate person and he sparked my curiosity. It was nice that he wanted to share one of his favorite places with me.

"Great. It's also right next to a stone sculpture museum that I think you will enjoy. So around eleven?"

"Perfect."

"I'm looking forward to it."

"Me too."

I hung up the phone. A glimmer of excitement caused

my heart to flutter. Dating was fun. It used to be something that I dreaded because I was so insecure about how I looked, what he might think of me, and whether I might embarrass myself. But now it was more like an opportunity to explore.

With each new date I accepted, I felt my comfort zone growing wider and wider. The date actually sounded like it would be a lot of fun. I could wear casual clothes and I'd get some culture along the way—not to mention that Spence looked downright gorgeous in the pictures I'd seen. He had loose curls, olive skin, and eyes that were quite possibly the largest I'd ever seen. I couldn't wait to get my chance to look into them.

I did feel a little guilty because my date with Ben had gone well. But we weren't exclusive by any means, and I wasn't ready to simply pick a man and continue dating.

I wanted to fall in love, but if that wasn't possible, I was going to explore my options.

As I returned to work on my book I thought of the e-mail that Blue had sent. It was hanging out there in cyberspace waiting for a response. It left me unsettled to think of him sitting somewhere waiting for my response. Was he really as heartbroken as he claimed?

As much as I didn't want to be, I was intrigued by his big secret. I wanted to know what it was—if it even really existed.

CHAPTER 18

I woke up early the next morning to get my writing done before my date with Spence. Since I'd shifted careers and become a writer I didn't always follow a set schedule. I had taken full advantage of being able to sleep in as late as I pleased.

As I began to write I got lost in an active scene. By the time my eyes were blurry, it was already after ten. I hadn't eaten breakfast, showered, or done anything but type.

I rushed around, glad that I could dress casual for this date. I was out the door, only a few minutes behind schedule.

The food cart was exactly as I'd imagined it would be. It smelled like grease, the counter looked less than clean, and the person selling the food acted put out that he had customers. Still, I couldn't wait to try the food.

Since my diet had gotten so much healthier, food carts hadn't been an option for me. But indulging now and then was fine, and I was looking forward to it.

The man standing beside the cart distracted me from

visions of a dripping cheese steak. He was shorter than I'd pictured, but just as handsome. He turned to look at me with a wide smile. I smiled in return as I walked up to him.

"Spence?"

"Only if you're Samantha." He grinned.

"I am." I offered him my hand to shake it. Instead he grasped it with a delicate touch and drew it to his lips.

After a flutter of a kiss, he released it.

I giggled. It was a sweet gesture, but unexpected.

"Are you hungry?" He wiggled his eyebrows.

"Absolutely!"

"My favorite is the Italian beef. I don't know if that's something that you would like. You're not one of those veggie chicks are you?"

I raised an eyebrow at the description. "I don't think so." I did my best to ignore the fact that I thought his words were a little insulting. I might not have chosen to go completely plant-based with my diet, but I had respect for those who did. Dieting was hard, no matter what you ate.

"Good. Then I'll get us two?"

"I can get my own—"

"No. Sorry. I know, women are all evolved and such, but if you're on a date with me, I'm paying." He maneuvered past me to place the order.

One of my eyes twitched.

Cool it, Sammy, he's just trying to be chivalrous—trying and failing.

Before I could get wrapped up in an internal argument he turned to look at me again.

"A beer maybe?"

"No thanks. I'll just have a water."

"You're not a drinker?"

"Not at eleven in the morning." I laughed, but stopped abruptly when I saw a beer in his hand. "I mean—it's just not for me."

He didn't seem to notice my discomfort. He paid for the order and carried the plates to a rickety wooden table and chairs. When I sat down across from him, I was reminded of why I'd agreed to a date with him. When he looked at me, his eyes were endless—the type that I could easily get lost in.

"So what do you do?"

"I'm a writer." I took a bite of the Italian beef and nearly cried out with pleasure. Luckily I managed to plant a napkin over my mouth before I did.

"A writer?" He quirked an eyebrow. "Like, one of those blog thingies?

"Well, I do have a blog. But I'm also working on a novel."

"Oh." He nodded. "Interesting. So I guess you're hoping to snatch up somebody with a real job, huh?"

My jaw dropped. My mouth just happened to be stuffed with Italian beef at the time. I chewed and swallowed so fast that I bit the side of my tongue.

"Excuse me? Why would you say something like that?"

"Relax, relax." He chuckled. "I just wanted to see if you're cute when you're mad."

I stared at him. I wasn't sure if I should shout at him or laugh at him. He must have mistaken my silence for my waiting for the results of his test.

"Yes—very cute."

"Wow, does that work on the women you date?" I shook my head.

"I don't know. Did it work on you?" The amount of charm in his smile made me forget just what I was angry about.

"What do you do, Spence?"

"I'm a truck driver—just local deliveries. I also do some painting."

"Oh? An artist?"

"I don't know. I like painting. I especially like painting portraits."

"That's really interesting." I smiled.

"Maybe you'd like to model for me some time?"

I couldn't tell if he was being sleazy or genuine. Spence was hard to pin down.

"I'm sure you could find a more suitable model."

"I'm not asking anyone else." He met my eyes with an intense stare that made me feel as if he'd already stripped me down and slapped me on a canvas.

"Oh, so where are the sculptures?" My heart fluttered.

I didn't know how to take Spence. He was abrasive and seemed a bit volatile, but at the same time he oozed sensuality. There was plenty of chemistry between us, which was enjoyable, but confusing.

"Right over there." He gestured to a large iron gate.

Stepping into the outdoor museum made me feel as if I was stepping back through time. I imagined being in ancient Rome, or a mystical place like Atlantis. The stone sculptures towered above me at heights nearly as high as the trees. And there were some as small as mice gathered around the oddest shaped triangle I'd ever seen.

"Isn't it stimulating?" Spence stared at the circle of stone. "It makes my mind spin trying to figure out what it is—what it's supposed to be."

"It's unique."

We strolled through the sculptures. Spence caught my hand in his and held it firmly. He did not let go the entire time we explored the museum. It was a little awkward for me, as I barely knew him, but he seemed content. When we finished our tour, he led me back to the entrance.

"Thanks for showing me this place. It's amazing. I probably never would have found it myself."

"It is amazing." He tugged me close, nearly knocking me off balance. "So are you."

"Uh, thanks." I tugged back from his grasp to create a more comfortable distance.

"What's wrong, Samantha?" He smiled at me. "I thought you had a good time."

"I did."

"So, let's make it even better." He tugged me close again and this time attempted to kiss me.

CHAPTER 19

I gave Spence a solid shove on his chest and ducked out of the way of the kiss. I couldn't deny that his desire for me inspired a desire of my own, but I didn't like how aggressive he was being.

"Sorry, I think you have the wrong idea about me, Spence."

"Oh, you don't like to have fun? Don't like to experience new things?"

"I like both of those things but that doesn't mean I want to move that fast." I shook my head. "I like to get to know a person a little first. Is that too old-fashioned for you?"

He shrugged and ran his hand back through his hair. "If that's what you want. I guess it's okay. I'm just not used to it."

"Well, then, it'll be something new. Don't you like trying new things?" I grinned.

He winked at me. "You got me. So we'll do this again?"

I almost declined. Spence was just a little too handsy for me. But then I reminded myself that this was all about trying to expand my experiences. Spence was interesting, he was a type of man I'd never dated before and most of all, he wasn't Blue—which was what I needed at the moment.

"Sure." I smiled.

After leaving Spence at the museum, I headed back to my apartment. I had plans with Max in a few hours and I wanted to change into something that was less casual. My mind was still on Spence and what might have happened if I'd let him kiss me.

The truth was that he stirred a strong want in me. I was never the type of girl to move fast in a relationship, but Spence sure made me question whether it was time for a change.

Despite the fact that I had a week full of dates planned, meeting Max for drinks was the highlight of my day. I couldn't wait to see him. I enjoyed drinking with Max. He was just about the only person that I would let go and have fun with. I trusted that he wouldn't tease me about anything embarrassing that I did, and that he would make sure I got home okay on the rare occasion that I'd had one too many drinks.

When I arrived at the little bar down the street from my apartment, Max was already there waiting for me.

"Hi." He smiled brightly at me as he stood up from

his bar stool. "I took the liberty of ordering us our first round."

"Thanks." I gave him a quick hug, then sat down on the bar stool beside his. "I've been looking forward to this all day."

"Really?" He glanced over at me. "Even with your date today?"

"Oh yes! Definitely." I laughed.

"Uh-oh, what happened?" He raised an eyebrow.

"It's more like what would have happened if I let it." I giggled and sipped my drink.

"Wait, what?" He leaned in a little closer. "Wasn't this your first date with this guy?"

I fixed him with an amused look. "You're judging me?"

"No, I'm just waiting for the details."

"His name is Spence. He's pretty hot." I took another sip of my drink.

"Hot?" Max sneered. "Probably one of those guys with more hair gel than hair."

"Hm." I winked at him. "No hair gel needed. In fact, he's got this natural allure to him. I can't explain it. With Ben, I couldn't really think about kissing him, but Spence—" I cleared my throat and finished my drink.

"Spence what?" Max scooted a little closer.

I noticed that he was dangerously close to tipping over his bar stool. I gestured to the bar tender for another drink. Then I put my foot on Max's bar stool to keep him from tipping over.

"I don't know. He's just one of those macho guys that bleeds sexy."

"Huh." Max narrowed his eyes. "Just how sexy?"

"Trust me, if I'd given him the green light, things would have gotten hot and heavy pretty fast. I had to put him in his place a few times."

"Doesn't sound very respectful." Max downed the rest of his drink.

"Maybe not, but I have to admit, I enjoyed it. It's ridiculous, right?"

"Yeah." He met my eyes. "It is."

I stared at him for a second. I expected him to smile to break the harshness of his words. He didn't.

"Here you go." The bartender set my drink down in front of me.

As the awkward silence grew between Max and me, I took a sip. I thought over my words and wondered if I'd said anything to upset him.

"I was being safe. We were in a public place with lots of people around." I shrugged. "If he had been any more aggressive I would have left."

"So a little disrespect is okay with you?" Max shook his head. "You should have higher standards than that."

"I think there's a gray area between disrespect and seduction. I mean, if you were with a woman and you really wanted to kiss her—but she wasn't showing interest—would you just ignore the desire?" I looked over at him.

Max only stared at his drink, so I continued. "You would probably touch her cheek, compliment her, find ways to get closer to her—you know—try to coax her into it, right? That's not really disrespectful."

"I don't know." Max swirled the liquid in his glass. "I guess I think a woman has a right to decide when she wants to be touched—when she wants to be approached in a romantic way."

"Max, you can't be serious."

"Why not?" He raised an eyebrow.

"Pamela Grant."

"Huh?" He looked away. "Wow, haven't thought about her for a long time."

"You seriously stalked her like a lovesick puppy."

"It wasn't stalking exactly."

"You told me, if you just had the chance to kiss her, you knew that she would fall for you."

"Well—uh—I was younger then."

"Hm. You got your kiss, didn't you?"

"And a bloody nose." Max rubbed his nose as if it still hurt.

"Well, if Spence crossed any lines, he'd get one too." I smiled. "You don't need to worry about me, Max. Things are finally going well. At least I'm not crying on your shoulder over Blue."

"Right." He finished his drink. "So you decided you're done with him?"

"Well." I sighed. "I should be."

"But?"

"I don't know. I just can't seem to stop thinking about him."

CHAPTER 20

Max ran his hands across the top of the bar. "Maybe it's worth giving Blue another shot."

"Wow, I didn't expect you to say that. You think Spence is a jerk. Blue stood me up—again—and you think I owe him another chance?"

"I didn't say that. You don't owe him anything. I just mean if you can't stop thinking about him, maybe there's something there."

"Maybe." I thought about it for a moment. Max always knew what I was really feeling even when I didn't know myself.

"Think about it." He shrugged. "Now, about Spence."

"I have another date with him. We'll see how it goes."

"And Ben?"

"Ben really seems pretty perfect. I have another date with him too. I'm looking forward to it. I just hope that I can connect with him."

"Hm." Max signaled for another drink. I looked at

him with surprise. He was drinking more than usual.

"Thirsty tonight?"

"A bit."

"Oh, Maxy Poo, are you drowning your sorrows?" I fluttered my eyes at him.

He turned to look at me and laughed. "Unless you've got a raft."

"I can be your raft." I winked at him. "I come equipped with floatation devices."

The moment the words came out of my mouth, I realized I might have had too much to drink.

Max laughed even louder. "Hm, I feel so much safer now. Shall we go for a swim?"

"Might want to check for leaks first." I nearly choked on my drink as I laughed around my words.

"Is that an invitation?" Max leaned toward me, flexing his hands.

"Max!" I leaned back in reaction to his approaching hands.

Of course I'd forgotten that my feet were on the rung of his bar stool. I tipped the whole thing over and Max landed in the arms of the woman sitting on the other side of him.

"Oops, sorry!" Max grinned at her.

"Oh no!" I tried to be horrified, but I was laughing too hard.

"I think your girlfriend is drunk." The woman shook her head.

"She's not my girlfriend, she's my floatation device!"

The woman shook her head again and moved to another seat.

"Max, shush, you're going to get us in trouble!"

"Me?" Max laughed. "I think you just proved to me that Spence could easily end up with a bloody nose. You're pretty good at protecting your personal space."

I laughed too and the natural comfortable energy ignited between us again. Whatever was going on with Max that made him act a little weird, I was okay with it. Just like he was okay with me knocking him off his bar stool. We understood each other in a way that not many friends seemed to.

I woke up the next morning feeling a little gun-shy after my date with Spence. Sure, he had gotten me fired up in a way that I hadn't been lately, but there were also some qualities that I didn't enjoy.

On Sunday I had an adventure date lined up. I was a little surprised when Kevin selected me as a match on MatchMe. He was extremely fit and active. Most of the time, it seemed that men who were very physically fit tended to want the same thing in a mate. Still, I figured it was worth a shot.

Kevin offered to take me to his favorite rock-climbing wall. It was not exactly my cup of tea, but I always liked to challenge myself. Rock climbing was one thing that hadn't even made my bucket list.

Sunday morning I woke up with a hint of dread. So many things could go wrong. I started to wonder why I'd agreed to the date in the first place. Then I remembered. Blue. I needed to get him out of my head.

I picked out some workout clothes and tried to make my hair look cute, although I knew as soon as I started sweating it would be a mess. I ate a very light breakfast and then headed out to meet Kevin.

Kevin's profile was full of pictures of his abdominal muscles and his chest, and there was even one that showed off his hipbones and nearly everything else. There was no question that he was in perfect shape. I suspected that maybe his pictures had been altered—or that they were old pictures.

Why would a man like Kevin need to go on MatchMe? It just didn't make sense to me.

So half out of curiosity and half out of interest, I showed up at the rock-climbing building.

When I stepped inside, I was greeted by the scent of sweat and disinfectant. The building was as big as a warehouse, with an assortment of walls to climb. There were also other obstacles to overcome and a course in the middle of the structure.

I looked around for any sign of Kevin. There were plenty of people in spandex, but none looked like Kevin to me.

"Samantha! Up here!"

I looked up to the ceiling. Kevin was at the very top of the tallest rock wall in the building. "I'll be right down!"

I cringed as he rappelled down to the ground. Once his harness was off he jogged over to me. He was every bit as solid as his profile picture had indicated.

"What do you say, Samantha, are you ready to change your life?" His smile was so eager that I could almost count all of his teeth.

CHAPTER 21

I looked up at the towering rock wall. "Uh, sure."

"Wow, great enthusiasm." He clapped his hands.

The sound was so sharp and unexpected that I jumped. It was clear to me that Kevin was passionate about rock climbing.

"I'll get JoJo to get you all set up."

JoJo was almost identical to Kevin, aside from having brown hair instead of blond. The two high-fived as Kevin walked up to him.

"JoJo, this is the girl I've been telling you about."

I raised an eyebrow. We barely knew one another, so I had no idea what he would have told JoJo about me.

"Hi." JoJo beamed at me. "Are you ready to change your life?"

I looked between the two of them. I didn't see any indications of religious belief, so I guessed they didn't intend to convert me.

"I'm ready to try rock climbing if that's what you mean."

"Right!" Kevin slapped me rather roughly on the

back.

I shot a glare in his direction. "Watch it!"

"Oh, sorry—don't know my own strength." Kevin laughed and flexed his arm to show me his muscle.

I tried not to be impressed. I really did, but it looked like a little mountain on his arm.

"You can touch it." He smiled.

"That's okay, I'm good." I tried not to laugh.

Kevin's behavior was strange to me but he appeared to be quite pleased with himself. Maybe his fitness obsession was the reason he was on a dating site.

JoJo began to help me get into a harness. When he tightened it there wasn't much room left for air.

"Are you okay?" Kevin looked into my eyes. "Are you ready for this?"

"I guess." The harness felt pretty uncomfortable in places that I didn't want to point out.

"Great! Great attitude! Up high!" He raised his hand into the air.

I stared at him for a minute before I realized he was expecting me to high-five him. Was this guy serious? I didn't want to be rude, so I slapped his hand. Then I pretended that it didn't hurt. Even his palm was rock solid.

"Let's go, Samantha! This is the first day of your new life!"

As he started to climb up the wall I suspected that he hadn't selected me for a date at all. He quite possibly had selected me to be his own personal project.

I tried to follow him up the wall, but getting my toes not to slip off the rocks was harder than I expected.

"You can do it, Samantha!" JoJo coached me. "Just stay focused and remember, nothing will feel as good as getting to the top!"

"Let's go, Samantha, get moving!" Kevin tried to motivate me, but he only inspired more annoyance.

I managed to climb up a few feet. My body trembled from using muscles that I didn't normally use. I felt the intensity of having the ground so far beneath me. I really didn't think I was going to make it to the top.

"Go, Samantha, go!" JoJo called out from below me.

"I'm going!" I snarled. All of the cheering was wearing on my patience.

"That's right, Samantha, use that anger!" Kevin plowed right up to the top of the rock wall.

I spent the rest of my journey to the top staring at his rear end. It wasn't exactly an unpleasant sight. However, his persistent encouragement ruined it for me.

"Oh, you're going to see some anger alright." My mind filled with visions of swinging him around on his harness like a tetherball.

I pushed myself harder to get to the top—the main reason being so that I could then get myself back down to end this ridiculous date.

By the time I reached the top, I was covered in sweat. The one positive thing so far was the fact that I'd gotten my workout in.

"Look at you! You should be so proud! I'm proud! Are you proud?"

I don't know what he might have seen on my face, but whatever it was made him get very pale and quiet very fast.

"Alright, Samantha, come back down!" JoJo waved from the bottom of the rock wall.

I hadn't really thought about the going-down process. Going up seemed like the hard part. But when I looked down from the height of the ceiling my stomach lurched. I was glad I hadn't eaten too much for breakfast.

"You can do it—"

"Stop it!" I scowled at Kevin. "Just stop."

Kevin looked a bit like a smacked puppy.

I gritted my teeth and began to make my way slowly down the rock wall.

You can do this, Samantha. All you have to do is get to the bottom. Everything is going to be fine—just a little rough patch—and then you'll be back on your feet.

Except I didn't feel anything under my feet. In fact, my feet were no longer on the rock wall and I was falling. JoJo pulled on the harness to slow my descent, and the harness got a little too familiar with my nether regions.

"Ouch!" I grimaced. Kevin, who'd climbed down alongside me, reached out and grabbed my hand. I was actually glad he did. He eased me to the ground.

"You okay?" he frowned.

"Get this thing off of me!" I tugged at the straps of the harness.

JoJo went to work unbuckling. I was a little concerned that I might need a surgical removal.

Once the harness was off, I actually did feel proud. When I looked up at the rock wall I'd just climbed, I was impressed that I'd done it.

"You're pretty strong." Kevin patted my back.

I tried not to bark at him. "Thanks. So are you." I pretended not to be having visions of him being tossed off the side of a rock wall.

"I know that it's customary on a date to go out for a meal, but I want to introduce you to something even better."

I was covered in sweat and sore in unmentionable places. I didn't have the will left in me to argue with him.

"Okay."

CHAPTER 22

Kevin led me over to the juice bar at the other side of the building. I didn't mind that too much. I'd gone through a juicing phase and some of the concoctions could be really delicious. I looked over the menu and was about to select a drink when he ordered for me.

"We'll both have the Green Machine."

"Oh, what's in that?"

"Only the most nutritious experience of your life!"

I looked at the glass of green sludge that was placed on the counter in front of me. "Oh."

"Drink up! The texture is a little hard to get past, but try to think about what it's doing for your body and how it will transform you from the inside out!"

"Look, Kevin, I'm all about trying new things, but this is not going anywhere near my mouth." I frowned and met his eyes. "I appreciate what you're doing here, but if you're going to ask a girl out you really shouldn't be doing it to boost your personal training experience."

"I just thought we could get fit together!" He was still quite enthusiastic.

"Right—except you already have zero percent body fat. So really I'd be the one getting fit."

"Is something wrong with that?"

"Not at all. But I'm not interested in a man who wants to change me. Either you take me for who I am right in this moment—not who you think I might one day be—or you don't."

"But, Samantha, you have so much potential."

"I know I do. I'm working on my health and I will continue to, but not for any man. For me. Kevin, I'm sure you'll find someone who is interested in your version of dating, but it isn't me."

"I'm sorry to hear that. I thought you were ready for transformation."

"What I'm ready for is a shower and an ice pack to sit on. I'm not forcing my transformation. I'm letting it happen naturally. It may take longer than your brand, but in the long run, I'm transforming my life, not just my body."

"Fair enough." Kevin sighed. "Is there any chance you'd want to do a short testimonial that I could put on my website?"

"Bye, Kevin."

As I walked—or more accurately, waddled—out of the building, I was glad to leave Kevin behind. He might have had the body of a god, but his personality was more akin to a goldfish's.

I opened the door to my apartment and let out a groan as I stepped in. My entire body was already throbbing with pain from the workout. All I could think about was getting into a hot bath. I stripped down and ran the water.

As I rubbed at the muscles in my legs, I thought about my body. I could admire Kevin's dedication to fitness and his flawless physique, but I didn't really want that for myself. I liked the softness of my body and thought my curves were sensual. I wanted to be healthier, but I didn't want to be skin and bone, or nothing but muscle.

I eased my body into the hot water with a sigh of relief. Even though I hadn't enjoyed the date that much, I had actually enjoyed the rock climbing. It was something I hadn't thought I could accomplish, but I gave it a shot, and managed to do it.

As I closed my eyes and relaxed, my mind filled with images of climbing mountains. In my fantasy, I was strong, I was healthy, and I was determined to get to the top. I was also not alone.

When I reached the top, I turned and smiled at the person who was climbing right behind me. The person I smiled at just happened to be Blue—my faceless Blue, who I could recognize just by emotion and energy.

All of the peace I'd summoned with my relaxing bath disappeared. My chest tightened with pain. I would never meet Blue. He would never be the one at my side as I accomplished my dreams. The thought brought tears to my eyes. It was nothing I ever believed would happen.

I climbed out of the tub and dried off. With just my robe on, I walked over to my computer. I had every right to be mad, to never speak to him again, but I just couldn't imagine the rest of my life without him. Maybe we would never be in love, but that didn't mean that I didn't miss his advice and support.

I sat down and began typing out an e-mail.

Blue,

I read your e-mail. I know that you think we can be more, but I no longer think that's a good idea. I want you to be part of my life. I honestly can't imagine not having you to talk to, but I will no longer put my heart on the line. I would love for us to continue our relationship as friends, but I have no interest in meeting you or in anything more than friendship. If you can put that behind us, then we can still have an amazing friendship. If you can't, I guess this will have to be goodbye. I hope that you are able to find the love that you are looking for.

Samantha

I read over the e-mail. I thought it sounded a little harsh. But that was okay. I was still angry. I had a right to be harsh.

I sent the e-mail and then took a deep breath.

Would Blue value our friendship enough to want to continue it?

LILLIANNA BLAKE

CHAPTER 23

I was still sore when I woke up the next morning. My muscles felt like the mountain had climbed me rather than the other way around. My emotions were off-kilter too, because I wasn't sure if I should have sent that last e-mail to Blue. I wanted him to know I cared, but I needed to draw that line in the sand for the sake of my own sanity.

As I got ready for my breakfast date with Ben, I tried to remind myself how much I'd enjoyed our last date. I hoped that this time I'd get to know him a little better and maybe find that spark that had been missing during our first date.

As I finished dressing my phone chimed with a text. I picked it up and smiled at Ben's sweet words.

I'm looking forward to our date this morning. See you soon.

It was nice that he was making such an effort to connect with me. He didn't leave me waiting or wondering whether he was thinking about me. I was sure that this would be the day that I would find that attraction to Ben that I'd hoped for. I sent back a quick text.

Me too. See you in 20.

I headed out for the date feeling much better than I'd felt since waking up that morning. I'd even forgotten to check to see if Blue had e-mailed me back. I didn't think about Blue until I was in my car driving toward the cafe that I'd chosen for my date with Ben. It overlooked a small lake and had a wonderful assortment of meals to choose from. It had been on my list of places to take Blue when we finally got together—which is probably why I was now thinking about Blue as I made my way to my date with Ben.

I liked the idea of seeing Ben first thing in the morning. I hoped he wouldn't be as nervous as he was last time.

He was already seated at one of the tables on the porch that overlooked the water when I arrived. I studied him for a few minutes from a distance. There was nothing about him that I could pinpoint as unattractive, and yet, I still saw him just as another person sitting there—not as the potential love of my life.

Give it time, Sammy.

I walked up the steps and joined him at the table.

"Good morning." He smiled brightly.

"Good morning." I sat down beside him so that he could still see the water.

He reached out as if he might rest his hand on mine, but then drew back.

I smiled and took his hand. "How are you this morning?"

I wanted to feel electricity when I touched him, but all I felt was a sweaty palm. I was sure mine was a little damp too.

"Great, now that you're here. You're right about this place being amazing."

We chatted for a few minutes before ordering. I did find it easy to talk to him, but I had to draw him into the conversation.

"So you mentioned your sister last time we were together. Are you two close?"

"Oh yeah, we were best friends growing up and still are. She's busy now, though, with a husband and kids."

"Yes, we're hitting that age, aren't we—where everyone is pairing up and parenting." I smiled.

"Sure—and to be honest, I can't wait to join in. I see her with her kids, and I have to admit, my biological clock starts ticking. But I'm sure you know all about that." He laughed.

I quirked an eyebrow. "Not exactly."

"Really? You're not ready to settle in and start a family?" He looked a little disappointed.

I started to sweat. I pulled my hand away from his and tried to cover my anxiety with a smile.

"Well, sure, I want those things—I think—but I'm

not in any rush."

"But there's only so much time."

"We still have plenty of time." I laughed.

"Sure, if you want to be raising kids into your sixties."

"How many kids?" I found it hard to breathe.

"Oh, I want a big family. Maybe six or seven kids."

"Uh, that's a lot." I widened my eyes. "I mean, why not just go for an even dozen?"

"I'm not opposed to that." Ben grinned.

I felt my uterus tighten into a tiny frightened ball. "Oh."

"Don't worry, I'm just kidding." He shook his head. "I would like a big family, but you know, it comes down to what feels right."

I laughed with relief. But he brought up some good points. I was searching for true love, but I hadn't really thought about the steps that came after. Would the person I found love with be a suitable partner for the rest of my life?

"Have you ever been close to that step?"

"Once. At least I was. Looking back, I know now that she wasn't. You know, it should be simple. You meet someone, share the same views, similar goals—you get married and have a family."

"I wish it was that simple." I laughed.

"Why can't it be?"

I met his eyes and realized he was serious. There was no magic in love for Ben. It was a game of numbers. If everything lined up, then it was the perfect match. I grew a little uneasy as I realized he was likely calculating my potential. I couldn't help but wonder how I added up.

By the end of our date, I still felt very little spark with Ben, but when he invited me out again, I accepted. Ben was nice, respectful and I had no doubt that he would make an excellent father.

Maybe he was on to something. Maybe it was more important to look at a future spouse from a logical perspective than a romantic perspective. I had to wonder if it was an idea worth exploring.

CHAPTER 24

The entire drive home, I tried to convince myself that a relationship without passion could work too. Scenes from romance novels I'd read over the years and romantic movie scenes played out in my mind. Without passion they were all lackluster. I just didn't see how I could spend the rest of my life with someone I had no real chemistry with. I was sure that passion could fade over the years, but to start out a relationship with zero spark? I shuddered at the idea.

At my apartment I headed straight for my computer. I wanted to see if Blue had written me back. I felt a buzz of excitement when I saw that he had.

Samantha,

I don't even know how to say this, but no.

My heart dropped. He didn't even want to be friends? My vision blurred for a moment with panic. I blinked a few times and continued to read.

I know it's not fair of me, but I can't just be your friend. I can't accept that I will never get to meet you. Samantha, if you give me another chance I can make everything right, or at least give you an explanation that you can understand. I have no right to ask, but I'm not asking—I'm begging. I need the opportunity to set things straight. Please, will you give me that chance?

Let me know if there is anything I can do to get you to agree. I will do it. No questions asked. Samantha, what we have is far too complicated for us to just abandon it. I need the opportunity to tell you the truth once and for all. I can't do that in an e-mail. It needs to be in person. I may not deserve it, but I need just one more chance.

Love,
Blue

I sat back and skimmed over his words again and again. I wanted to feel sympathy for him, but I didn't. I was angry. Angry that he would even ask me for another chance. I decided against typing a response, as I wasn't sure that he would survive it. My blood was boiling.

I stood up and began to pace around the apartment like a caged animal. I wished I could see him in person and tell him what I thought of his needing one more chance. But underneath all of that anger was desire.

It reassured me to know that he still wanted me, that he was willing to fight for me. But wasn't that just a fantasy? Blue, who claimed to be so interested in me, had yet to bother to meet me.

Ben had met with me twice in one week. He had a plan for the future, and no secrets to keep.

Maybe my lack of attraction to Ben had nothing to do with him and everything to do with my being attracted to the wrong kind of guys.

I was head-over-heels for Max. As I recalled our encounter in the garden, it made me dizzy.

Even though I hadn't met Blue, I longed for him.

I adored two men who were completely unavailable to me.

I paused in front of the mirror and shook my head at my own reflection. "Maybe it's you that's asking for the heartbreak, Sammy. Ben would never hurt you like that."

My phone began to ring. I grabbed for it and nearly tripped over my own feet in the process. My clumsiness was coming back, as was my insecurity.

"Hey, beautiful."

"I'm not beautiful."

"Okay. Hey, gorgeous."

"Oh, Max." I sighed. The last thing I needed was him plucking at my emotions with his kind words.

"What's wrong? Bad date?"

"No." I smiled. "Actually it was a great date."

"Oh?"

"Ben is wonderful. I set another date with him. In fact things are going so well that I think I'm ready to stop dating other people. Ben has all of the qualities that I'm looking for."

My confession was met with silence.

"Max, are you there?"

"I thought you had a date with that Spence guy?"

"I do. But I think I'll cancel it. I want to spend more time with Ben. He seems like he's really into the idea of commitment and moving forward in life. I'm ready for that."

"How?"

"What do you mean how?"

"How are you ready for that?" Max's voice was hard and louder than normal. "You just had your heart broken by Blue. You need time to heal. Or Ben is just going to be a rebound."

"Max, Ben can't be a rebound if I've never even met Blue. What is going on with you?"

"Sammy, I just think you're moving too fast. You barely know this guy."

"That's the point, isn't it? I want to get to know him. I don't see a reason to keep dating around if he is the one I'm interested in."

"Does he make you happy?"

"He's very nice."

"That's not an answer."

"Yes, it is. He shows up for our dates. He treats me with respect. He's a good man."

"Being a good man doesn't make him the right man

for you, Sammy."

"Who are you to lecture me on love?" I laughed a little to soften my words. But I meant them. I was annoyed that Max couldn't be happy for me.

"I'm not lecturing you, Sammy. I just—I don't know—I just think you should give it a little more time."

I sighed and closed my eyes. Max usually knew me better than I knew myself. Maybe he was seeing something that I wasn't.

"Alright, I'll give it more time. I don't even know if Ben wants to be exclusive."

"Good. Sammy, you know I only want what's best for you. You know that, right?"

"I do." My heart filled with warmth.

I did know that Max loved me in a sacred way that no one else would.

After I hung up with him, I decided that I needed to clear my head and my spirit. I hadn't been to meditation class in a long time. I thought it might help me get more clarity on my situation.

Luckily, I knew of one group that met that night. I was so caught up in listening to so many opinions that I could no longer hear my own.

I changed into something more comfortable and decided to try to write for a bit.

CHAPTER 25

When I arrived at the meditation class, the group was already seated. It was awkward to pick my way carefully between people and legs—some of which resembled pretzels—and attempt not to disturb those that were already chanting. Once I found an empty space I settled in.

All around me, I heard the breaths that people were drawing in and then releasing. It reminded me to breathe as well. I needed to calm my mind—to sort through all of the worries that had been thrust upon me—and all of the hurt. It had been some time since I'd heard that clear, still voice inside of me.

As the layers of my daily life began to fall away from my thoughts, images surfaced in my mind. There was an image of Max and the way he'd looked at me when he called himself dangerous, and then an image of Spence as he sought a kiss I wasn't ready for. Both ignited a different type of passion within me.

With Max, it was all longing—a deep desperation along with a hint of sadness, because I would never truly experience the desire I felt for him. With Spence, it was pure primal need—a need to be drawn into wild euphoria without thought for consequences.

As those two images subsided, there was a ripple of blue light. It didn't need a face or even a name. It caressed me on the inside. It touched my deepest emotions. It awakened an urge to blend energies. I recognized it and it recognized me…on a metaphysical level.

I opened my eyes with a jolt to find everyone in the room staring at me, including the man who was running the class. I assumed from the intense visuals that I'd experienced that I had fallen asleep and perhaps begun snoring. However, the flushed cheeks and mildly horrified expressions concerned me.

"Are you okay?" A woman beside me reached out and touched my wrist.

"I'm sorry. Did I fall asleep?"

My question was met with silence. A few people looked in my direction but quickly looked away. I wondered what I'd done to draw so much attention and elicit such a strange reaction.

The woman beside me leaned close and whispered in my ear. "Do you do guided meditations? Because I'd love to go on that journey with you."

"What?" I frowned. "What exactly are you talking about?" My heart started to beat just a little faster than normal as I waited for her response, but I didn't have time to press her for more information before the class instructor was interrupting our conversation.

"Class, sometimes when we have a deeply moving spiritual experience, it awakens all aspects of us— spiritual, emotional, and sexual." He looked right at me.

My eyes widened. Was I being sexually harassed by a meditation teacher?

"It's perfectly natural to experience your urges intensified by the connection to the universe. I'm sure that it was very liberating for you, Samantha, wasn't it?"

No. No. I refused to believe it.

"I don't know." I frowned. "I thought I fell asleep."

"You were groaning like a beast!" Someone in the back of the room finally revealed the truth to me.

"I was not!" I stood up. "I think I would know if I was."

"We all heard it." Another man grinned at me.

My face was hot. "I'm sorry if I interrupted you."

I tried to get past the folded legs that surrounded me. Every step I took seemed to lead to another appendage to trip over. I was nearly to the door when someone nearby decided to stretch out their legs. I caught my foot beneath their calf and face-planted into the pretzeled legs of the meditation teacher.

"Oh, well, that was unexpected." He cleared his throat—which in the meditation world was akin to screaming in horror.

I jumped up and nearly fell back over a woman who'd leaned forward in an attempt to catch me. I managed to catch my balance and did a little pirouette right out the door of the classroom.

Once outside, I laughed with embarrassment but also with relief.

I had my answer.

I needed that passion in my life. My body craved it, as did my spirit.

The question was, could I have it with Ben?

I realized that during the meditation Ben hadn't even entered my thoughts. Maybe the problem was that I had too many romantic loose ends roaming around in my mind.

There was Max, who I'd come to understand would always be there in some way. Then there was Blue, who, despite our rocky relationship lately, apparently stirred the deepest desire in me. No wonder I felt no spark with Ben. There wasn't any left for him!

As I walked back to my apartment, I made a decision. Before I could move forward with Ben, I needed to end things with Blue.

CHAPTER 26

I sat in front of the computer for what felt like hours. Really, it was probably more like twenty minutes. I agonized over exactly what I wanted to say to Blue. I didn't want to give him false hope or set myself up for another disappointment.

I took a deep breath and remembered the way I'd experienced the sensation of him during my meditation. This wasn't just an e-mail, it was a letter to perhaps the only man that would ever make me feel that way.

Dear Blue,

I mean that. You are dear to me in ways I can't begin to explain.

You don't deserve another chance. You have hurt me with what I can only assume has been a manipulative game.

Of course my heart wants to believe that there is some kind of reasonable explanation for your behavior, but my heart seems to be getting me into trouble these days.

It may not be the wisest choice on my part, but the truth is that you're stopping me from being able to move forward with a man who I believe would treat me very well. He deserves my affection and attention, but I can't give it to him, because when I close my eyes, it's you that I see. When I feel a touch on my skin, it's yours. When I feel my heart flutter, it's because of thoughts of you.

It is embarrassing for me to admit all of this, but you need to understand that I am not interested in just you.

Blue, you have become a part of me—a part of my life and a part of every date I have with any other man.

I will give you one more chance. Not for you, but for me.

You must understand the impact your game will have on me if you decide not to show up again. I'm not just some faceless stranger on the other side of a computer. I'm a woman with a heart that is delicate and wide open.

One more chance. That's it.

Sunday night—six—at Shannon's. I'm sure you can look up the address.

Just be there.

Samantha

I didn't read it over. I'd taken so long to write each word that I knew them by heart. I wanted him to know that I was still angry, but I also wanted him to know how important he was to me. It was time to put all of my cards on the table. If he didn't show up, at least I'd taken the time to tell him how I really felt. It was intimidating, but I felt some relief for having spilled it all.

Then anxiety began to creep in—about whether he would respond, whether he would show, whether or not he really was some sadistic man giggling at my obsession. Of all the aspects of falling in love that I'd focused so much on, risk wasn't one that I'd really thought about. Now I knew that giving my heart to someone was possibly the most dangerous act I'd ever committed. It reminded me of what Max had said to me in the garden after Blue had stood me up.

Curiosity certainly could be dangerous.

Later that day I tried to work on my book. The romance part was a huge stumbling block. In fact, I was at the point that it made me angry to even work on it. I felt like I was selling lies to my readers about what love was like. How could I write it without firsthand experience? Then I realized that there were tons of romance writers out there. I didn't think that all of them had experienced romance in this way either.

The writing group that I'd joined was focused more on refined literature. Maybe I could find a group that was just for romance writers. I might be able to get some great ideas from them.

I did a quick Internet search and found a group that met the next afternoon. I could go to the meeting before my date with Spence. It might even put me in a better mood to enjoy his company.

I was glad that Max had talked me out of hopping right into things with Ben.

I did feel that I needed to see where things might potentially go with Spence. He was rough around the edges, but I hoped that underneath he and I might have a deeper connection.

Before I went to bed, I checked my e-mail. I was surprised not to see anything from Blue. I felt like things were starting all over again. He was pulling back—not responding, even though I'd finally given him what he wanted. Then again, maybe he'd been put off by the harshness of my e-mail.

I went to bed with that battle going on in my mind.

When I woke up the next morning, I had to fight the urge to check my e-mail right away. I didn't want to be drawn back into the chaos of waiting for communication from Blue.

As I headed for my computer with a cup of coffee, my phone chimed.

I picked it up to see a message from Ben.

I'm looking forward to seeing you again soon. Just wanted to see how you're doing today? I hope you're having a great morning.

I smiled at the sweetness of the text. It meant a lot to me that Ben went out of his way to connect with me. As I went to text him back, I noticed that there was an e-mail from Blue on my computer screen. I got distracted and nearly dropped my phone into my cup of coffee. I managed to catch it right before it slipped into the hot liquid, but I mashed a few buttons in the process. I scowled at the computer screen as if Blue could see my displeasure. After all, it was his fault that I'd almost dropped my phone.

I sent a quick text back to Ben.

Thanks for the check-in. I'm looking forward to our date too. Thanks for the note. I hope you are having a great day too.

CHAPTER 27

I sat down and was about to open the e-mail from Blue when I received a text back. I smiled again at how responsive Ben was, but when I checked my phone the text was from Max.

We have a date?

I cringed as I realized that I'd sent the text to Max by mistake. I must have switched to his text log when I caught the phone.

So sorry, that was meant for Ben.

Oh, no good morning for me?

I laughed and shook my head. Between Ben, Blue, and Max, I was beginning to see that dating could be a bit of a juggle.

Good morning, Max. I hope you're having a great day.

I smiled as I sent the text.

Thanks. I am now.

He added a little heart emoticon. I tried not to roll my eyes. Max could be a little cheesy on the phone.

I turned back to my computer. The e-mail from Blue was short and sweet.

Samantha,

Thank you, thank you, thank you. I will be there. I know I've said it before, but I will be there. We will talk about everything then. Thank you for giving me another chance.

Blue

I frowned and wondered if I'd done the right thing. At least he'd responded.

I pushed the thought out of my mind and tried to write for a while.

Around midday I took a break to shower. I dressed for the writing group and the date that I'd head to after. The slip dress was a bit much for a writing group, but it would be nice for the date.

Spence had texted me to let me know that he was taking me on the Starlight Ferry. It was a ferryboat that ran the length of a local river and back with live music, a small dinner, and plenty of starlight. I'd always wanted to go on it, but had never had a date that wanted to go. Max had offered once, because he knew that I wanted to go, but it was not the type of thing you did with a best friend. It was far too romantic. I was pretty excited about experiencing it.

I could have sent a note back to Blue, but I decided against it. I was going to leave him alone until our date. I wanted him to prove himself by showing up, so I would leave no room for making excuses. Luckily, I had the writing group and the date with Spence to distract me from thoughts of Blue.

When I walked into the cafe, I noticed the group of people clutched together in a circular space dotted with couches and easy chairs. It was the perfect writers' nook. I smiled as I walked up to the group. I hoped that they would be a bit friendlier than the last group I'd joined. It appeared, however, that I'd walked right into the middle of an argument.

"It's ridiculous to use funny names for body parts. They are what they are. Why can't we just call them by their name?"

"That's nonsense. It breaks the spell. Romance, even erotic romance, is about fantasy. No woman wants an anatomy lesson in the middle of her smut binge."

"Oh, don't use that word." An older woman

scrunched up her nose. "That's so impolite."

"It is what it is." The younger woman shrugged. Then she looked up at me with a half-smile. "You must be Samantha."

"I am." I smiled in return. "Sorry to interrupt."

"Oh please do. I don't think the great anatomy debate can go on much longer without all of us losing our minds. Here, sit next to me." She gestured to an empty easy chair.

As I sat, I assessed the group. There were six people, not counting myself—three women and three men. One of the men looked to be in his late teens, another might have been in his forties, and a third's white hair indicated that he might be sixty or more. The three women looked to be about five to ten years apart in age. I was sure I'd get some good advice from people with such a variety of life experience.

"Samantha, since you're new we should probably let you talk first. This group gets off on a tangent and it could be hours before we bring up another topic."

"Thanks." I smiled at them. "I should tell you right off the bat that I'm not really a romance writer. However, there's an aspect of my book that is romantic. I'm having a hard time with this part, because, to be honest, I've never been in love—not the kind of love that I want to write about. I thought maybe you all could give me some advice on how to write this part of my book without having the personal experience."

All six of the people stared at me with some variation of amusement.

That was not the reaction that I'd expected. I started to wonder if I was in the wrong group.

The woman beside me placed her hand lightly on mine and smiled patiently. "Hon, you know that romance isn't real, right?"

"Excuse me?" I laughed a little.

None of their expressions changed.

"Samantha, what we write is fantasy." The man with white hair locked eyes with me. "It's not meant to be taken seriously. If I wrote about real romance, no one would read my books. No one wants to hear about the arguments or the day-to-day struggle of trying to make a relationship work. I mean, what love comes down to is a chemical misfiring of the brain that doesn't last."

CHAPTER 28

The man's words hit me hard. What hit me harder was that everyone in the group seemed to agree with him. The entire meeting of romance writers had nothing to do with romance and everything to do with how to sell people on a fantasy that none of them believed could ever be true.

I was more than a little disappointed.

"So none of you have been in love?"

"Oh sure, I've been in love." The youngest woman smiled. "I'm in love at least once a month."

"I thought I was in love, but it turned out that he was in love with my best friend." The woman beside me volunteered the information.

"I'm sorry that happened." I frowned.

This was not the inspiration I'd expected. In fact, I was tempted to tell my readers the truth—that no one had ever been in love.

"I was in love." The youngest man of the group spoke quietly. "It was amazing. But it didn't work out."

"Why not?" I met his eyes.

"Because she wasn't ready to settle down. We were too young, she said. Now she's married, with a baby on the way."

"You *thought* you were in love." The older man corrected him.

"So you don't believe that true love exists?" I looked around at each of them.

"Let's put it this way—if it exists, not everyone gets to experience it. That's what romance novels are for." The woman beside me smiled. "I hope we helped."

"Thanks."

I sat and listened for the remainder of the meeting, but it was hard for me to stay focused. I felt as if I was a kid again, discovering that Santa Claus wasn't real. I was a little annoyed that they all made their income selling something that they didn't even believe in. But I didn't really blame them either. It was clear that they'd learned from their own personal experiences.

After the meeting, I headed to my date with Spence. It still troubled me to think that I might have been looking for—hoping for—something that didn't even exist.

Maybe that was why Ben's way of looking at things was starting to make more sense to me. He wasn't waiting. He wanted to invest in a woman that he thought would make a good partner. He didn't care about being in love.

Maybe I needed to take a lesson from Ben.

Still, there was this deep desire in the pit of my stomach that I felt would never be fulfilled by just any man. It had to be the right person. Maybe I needed to be more open about who that right person might be.

I decided that I'd be a little more free with Spence on our date. Maybe if I gave passion a chance, I'd be able to find it.

The allure of live music could be heard as I walked up to board the ferryboat. My mind spun with anticipation. Maybe Spence was still not quite who I had in mind, but he had planned an amazing date.

"Ready?" He offered me his arm.

I slid my arm through his and we walked up a small metal ramp to the deck of the ship. There were other couples milling about the deck, but most were down below listening to the band.

As the ferry launched, I felt the rocking of the water beneath my feet. It was liberating to be disconnected from solid ground. I grabbed on to the railing and looked out across the water. Spence took the opportunity to drape his arm around my shoulders.

I braced myself. I knew that different types of people had different ways of showing their affection. Spence had only one way—with his hands. He leaned in close under the guise of looking at the moonlight.

I said, "It's beautiful."

"Not as beautiful as you in that dress." Spence pulled

me closer.

A light breeze off the water teased at my hair. He took the ruffle of tendrils as an invitation to nuzzle my neck. I tilted my head away enough to avoid his teeth.

"Spence, it's a nice night. Let's walk around the deck." I pulled away from him and began to walk.

Spence followed right after me.

"The boat's only out for so long. I figured we could add to it rocking."

I cringed at the crass words, but reminded myself that I was going to try to let passion happen between us.

"You're so funny, Spence." I leaned up and tentatively kissed him.

I had to admit that it felt strange to kiss him. It felt amazing in many ways, but it felt strange. I actually felt as if I was cheating. On whom, I wasn't sure. Blue? Ben? Myself?

I didn't have much time to think about it, as Spence had taken my kiss as a signal to let his hands roam the sensitive areas of my body.

When I felt a jolt of desire rush through me followed by a wave of mind-numbing need, I drew back sharply. I felt like I was getting a little out of control.

"Spence, wait." I pushed his hand away from the hem of the skirt of my dress. "That's a little fast for me."

"Oh, right, we should eat first." He grabbed my hand and whisked me into the dining room.

I was relieved to share the meal with him, as it meant

he wouldn't have his hands on me. I was also a little confused by the reaction of my body. Even though I wasn't sure if I even liked Spence, my body had been more than willing to participate in some kind of passionate something with him. If I hadn't stopped him—if I'd let myself go with the flow—I was sure it would have led to places I didn't expect to go on a boat in the middle of a river.

As soon as our meal was over, he led me out to a more private area on the deck.

"So, Spence, what are your dreams of the future?"

"The only thing I'm dreaming about is your skirt around your—"

"Wait, wait!" He already had me pinned back against the railing.

I remembered what Max had said about respect.

"What? We already had dinner." Spence looked annoyed.

"I'm sorry, Spence, but I'm just not going at your speed."

"Lighten up. It's the way of the world now, doll. Just relax and enjoy it. It's nothing to take so seriously."

"I do take it seriously." I met Spence's eyes. "I'm not interested in any flings."

"I guess we're not on the same page then. I live my life with passion. I don't want relationships. I want fun, and as much fun as I can get."

"If that's your idea of fun, that's great. My idea is a

little different."

"Knitting?"

"Getting to know a person. Connecting with them. Building a sense of trust and interest." I shrugged. "It's not something everyone enjoys."

"That's for sure. I wish you had told me that before we got on the boat." He frowned. "What a waste."

I was more than a little insulted by his words, but I did my best not to take it personally.

"Well, don't let me stop your fun. I'm sure you can find someone to share it with."

"Great." Spence winked at me and then walked off.

The boat had just made its turn to start back toward the dock. I sighed and looked up at the stars. At least the journey was beautiful, even if the experience hadn't been what I'd hoped for.

CHAPTER 29

After my disappointing date with Spence, I decided to become a recluse for a bit. I needed a little time to sit and really think about what I wanted.

For so long my main focus had been falling in love, but I hadn't really thought about the consequences of that. Once I found the man that I'd be with for the rest of my life, that would be it. There would be no more dating around. Over time, I'd be planning for marriage, possibly children, buying a house—the list was endless.

I did want all of those things, but had I been rushing something I wasn't ready for?

A part of me wished that I could be more like Spence and follow passion rather than emotion. But I couldn't imagine ever really enjoying that. I was sure that I needed to be with someone that I truly cared about and felt intense passion for.

I lay awake that night thinking about whether I could ever feel that way with Ben. I really wanted to.

The next evening was my date with Blue.

Blue, just the thought of whom had made a spectacle out of me in meditation class. Blue, who seemed to know every intimate detail about me, except for the fact that I didn't like being stood up. My heart raced when thoughts of him filled my mind.

I considered not going. It would serve him right to be stood up. But I knew that I wouldn't be able to resist.

For the longest time Max had been my one great love. Now I had Blue, who kept insisting he felt the same way. I wasn't willing to miss out on the chance to find out.

It was difficult for me to sleep and it was difficult for me to climb out of bed the next day. By the time I got around to making breakfast my mind was blurry with emotion.

I decided to give Max a call.

"How'd it go last night?"

"Wouldn't you like to know?"

"Yes I would, actually."

I smiled a little. Max sounded just a tad jealous. It reminded me that he was the one I truly wanted to be with. But I stifled that desire quickly. Max wasn't an option for me.

"I tried to enjoy myself."

"Enjoy yourself?"

"Yes. You know—relax, have fun, be a little bit more like you."

"Oh, God."

"Don't worry. I didn't succeed. Spence and I will not

be going out again. But the stars were beautiful."

"I'm glad."

"About what?"

"That you stayed true to yourself."

"You sound like a Hallmark ad."

"You know I'm right. So what are you doing today?"

I paused. I hadn't spoken much about my date with Blue to Max. But now I needed him to be my backup yet again.

"I have a date."

"With who?"

"Blue."

"Oh? When?"

"At six. So I might need some moral support when he doesn't show up again."

"That's not exactly the positive attitude I'm used to."

I frowned. "I don't know, Max. I'm starting to wonder if it isn't all a fantasy. I guess I'll find out tonight."

"I'll be there."

"Thanks, Max." I was relieved to know that he would be there for me if Blue stood me up.

I didn't spend a lot of time getting ready. I threw on a comfortable sundress. I applied a smattering of make-up. I kept reminding myself not to get my hopes up. All my non-fuss paid off when, at five after six, I sat all alone at a table at Shannon's.

It was like déjà vu.

The minutes ticked by, one by one, like a sickening march to my heartbreak. I felt the stares from other people around the restaurant. I saw two of the waitresses whispering to one another. It could have been about anything, but of course, I thought it was about me.

I sank down in my chair. I expected tears to come, but they didn't. I was too hurt to even summon them.

In the back of my mind, as if I was determined to be as foolish as possible, I still hoped that he was just running late—running late after I'd made it clear to him that this was his last chance.

I tapped my fingers lightly on the back of my phone. I thought about calling Max or texting him. But I didn't want to. I didn't want him to know that it had happened again. He was just one more way for me to fool myself into believing that I deserved love. For all of his pretty words about how much he cared about me and how beautiful he thought I was, he would never return my desire for him. Wasn't he about the same as Blue in that way?

I glanced at the time on my phone. Ten minutes late. My heart ached. Why had I done this to myself again? I thought about Spence. Maybe I'd missed my chance. Maybe I should have let him have his fun with me. At least I would have gotten a little something out of that.

Then there was Ben. Ben, who wanted a big family and a logical marriage.

I closed my eyes. I wished that the entire restaurant would disappear, that somehow I was stuck in the middle of a nightmare. Instead, when I opened my eyes I saw what I thought must be a hallucination.

CHAPTER 30

Max was there, standing a few feet away from my table. He stared at me from where he stood and didn't take a step closer. A few people looked in his direction. A waitress walked toward him. That let me know that he was actually there. But he didn't look away from me. How had he known? Had he been outside watching?

"Max." I smiled at him despite the pain that was consuming me.

"Sammy." He avoided the waitress and walked toward my table.

All at once, I was relieved of the embarrassment of being stood up. The rest of the people in the restaurant had no idea that Max was not there as my date. He was there as my best friend and he didn't want me to be alone. He sat down in the chair across from me. He hadn't smiled yet.

I figured he was angry that Blue had stood me up again.

"It's what I expected." I shrugged.

"It is?" His lashes spread, revealing his beautiful eyes.

"Sure. I mean, I hoped that he would show, but I didn't really expect him to." I looked down at my hands, which I noticed were shaking a little. I folded them up to hide the tremor.

"But he did." Max spoke in such a quiet voice that I was sure I hadn't heard him correctly.

"What do you mean?" I looked toward the window. "Did you see him out there?"

"Sammy." Max shifted in his chair. He leaned forward and reached for my hand.

I drew back away from him. I didn't want him to know that I was trembling in an attempt to hold back the grief that was brewing in me.

"He saw me and changed his mind—is that it?" I bit into my bottom lip.

"No, that's not it. Sammy, please." He reached for my hand again.

This time when I tried to dodge it, he grabbed my hand anyway. He tightened his grip when I tugged back.

I stared into his eyes with confusion. "I'm okay, Max. It's okay. It's what I expected. We should just go."

"No." He refused to let go of my hand.

I felt the electricity bolt through me in response to his touch. It was rather sadistic. Between the pain I was feeling over Blue's rejection and the desire that Max was forcing me to feel, I was sure that I would lose my mind right there in the middle of the restaurant.

"Sammy, I need to tell you something, but I don't

know if I'm brave enough."

I froze. I remembered that exact statement from an e-mail that Blue had written. As my mind began to react to that, Max looked into my eyes.

"Max, you know you can tell me anything. What's wrong?"

He licked his lips and looked down at the table. He seemed very troubled by what he wanted to confess.

"Max, I love you." I squeezed his hand. "Remember?"

"Do you?" He looked up at me.

When our eyes met, the spark that jolted through me stole my breath.

He continued, "I've done something—something I don't know that you're going to be able to forgive me for."

The waitress seemed to sense that we needed a moment. My mind raced with what Max could have done. I couldn't begin to imagine something that I'd not be able to forgive Max for.

"Just tell me." I searched his eyes. My heart lurched. "Does it have to do with our friendship?" My eyes burned with a mist of tears, because I'd always feared that one day something would happen that would take that from me.

"Yes."

Max's answer was so clear that it felt like a sword to my gut. He didn't even hesitate. It made me think that he'd been waiting to tell me this for some time. Why would he pick this moment of all moments, when I'd already been stood up by Blue, to talk about this with me? I tried to pull my hand away again, but he held it just as tight. A swirl of fury, hurt, and grief threatened to make me scream.

"I can't be friends with you any more, Sammy. I've tried. God, have I tried. I know that's what you want, but I just can't sit back and watch you dating these men. It makes me crazy and I—" His voice caught in his throat.

CHAPTER 31

In the cloud of all of my emotions, I could barely comprehend what he was saying. I could only stare at the tension in his expression. Maybe I understood perfectly. Maybe I was just too afraid to believe that it could be true.

"I thought that if you had the chance to get to know me—to see me as someone other than your buddy Max—I thought it might change how you feel. It seemed like every time I tried to get you to look at me in a different way, you would pull even further back. Blue could tell you the truth and you drew closer instead. But I let it get out of hand. I never meant to hurt you, Sammy. I'm so sorry that I did that. It broke my heart to see you with tears in your eyes. I was just so scared it would ruin everything if I told you the truth and I'd let things go on too long and I just didn't know how to fix it." He spoke so fast that I could barely keep up.

"Max, what are you saying?" I wondered for a moment if my mind had broken and I was hearing words that he wasn't actually speaking. It was the only explanation that made sense to me. "I don't understand."

I was starting to, but I still held my breath. I wanted to believe that it was true, but how could everything that I'd hoped for, for so long, suddenly be happening?

He clenched his jaw. He closed his eyes. Then I watched those beautiful lips part.

"Blue didn't stand you up tonight. He was just a little late. I'm right here." He opened his eyes and looked into mine. "I'm Blue."

My sight grew sharp. It was as if a veil had been lifted and I could see clearly for the first time. That swirl of Blue that I'd experienced in my meditation settled right into Max. I realized that how I felt about Blue was nearly identical to how I'd always felt about Max. Max, the true love that I never thought could be mine.

"Max." I breathed his name as if I was saying it for the first time. My world felt as if it had been flipped upside down in the most magical way. "Why didn't you just tell me?" I stared with disbelief across the table at him. "Didn't you know that I would do anything to hear you say that you wanted more than friendship? You had to have known."

I thought about all of the times that I'd come so close to kissing him, to telling him the truth about how I felt. All of those moments I'd let pass me by, because I was sure he could never feel that way about me.

"I did know." Max settled his hands in his lap. "For a

while I knew. I knew, but I thought I wasn't good enough for you. I wanted fun, not commitment. I didn't want to hurt you. I just wanted things to stay the same—until I was ready to change them. I was so selfish."

I nodded a little, but I didn't speak. I didn't want him to stop talking.

"Then suddenly it seemed like you changed. Like you were done with me in that way. I thought I'd missed my chance. I dropped hints, but you kept ignoring them or pushing me away. It was like I couldn't get you to see me as anything other than your friend any more. When I saw that you started a blog, I thought it might be my chance to communicate with you, to let you see who I really am. Not just this shallow womanizer, like you seemed to think, but that there was more to me." He shook his head. "It was only supposed to be for a little while, then I was going to tell you the truth. But the more I got to hear your thoughts, the more I shared mine with you and the more afraid I became that I would lose that connection with you if I told you the truth."

"How did I not know?" I stared at him with no expectation of an answer. I knew there wasn't one.

Max held my gaze. "I was careful."

"But why? Once you knew how I felt, why didn't you just tell me?"

"Because I was in too deep by then. I was afraid if I told you the truth you would never trust me again. I know how important that is to you."

"You know that, but you still did all of this."

I closed my eyes for a moment. I couldn't get anything to make sense. Amid all of my confusion, was pure bliss. Could it really be true?

"I just wanted you to know me—to know who I really am.

"Sammy, say something." I opened my eyes and looked at him intently. "Anything."

I parted my lips, but I couldn't form any words. My brain was still trying to catch up with my emotions.

"Sammy, I love you. I'm in love with you." He held my gaze as he spoke. "Tell me I'm not too late."

A ripple of pure euphoria carried through me. I still felt like I was in a dream—or worse, a psychotic break of some kind. I didn't really think any of it could be real.

Then all at once it struck me that it was real.

"Maybe I should go. Give you time to think."

He stood up from the table.

"No. Max, wait." I stood up and took his hand in mine. "Max, is this a dream?"

I almost didn't want him to answer. I didn't want there to even be a chance that this was all some cruel trick of my subconscious.

"It's real. I can prove it." He curled his fingers around my hand and pulled me close.

I could see him leaning close. I could feel the warmth of his lips as they neared mine. But I didn't believe it until I felt the tentative kiss. My heart leaped. My body quivered with the power of the electricity between us. He drew back some and looked into my eyes, as if waiting for my approval. I stared back at him, still too stunned to notice that we had the attention of everyone in the restaurant.

"Sammy?" Max squeezed my hand. "Is it too late? I'll understand if it is. I won't like it, but I'll understand."

I almost laughed at the absurdity of his words. How could it ever be too late for Max? I was about to tell him just that, when I felt a deep urge to do something that I hadn't thought I'd ever do.

CHAPTER 32

I couldn't resist it. I didn't want to put it off any longer.

"Wait. Wait, there's something I have to do!" I tugged my hand free of Max's and reached into my purse. He looked at me with tightened lips and narrowed eyes. It seemed as if he was bracing himself for my rejection.

"Just one moment," I mumbled and continued to dig until I felt the well-worn paper against my fingertips. It was so familiar to me that I didn't even have to see it to know that it was the right piece of paper.

Max watched as I pulled out my bucket list. He smiled as he recognized the paper with all of the different-colored ink, the doodles, and the marked-off items. One very important one, surrounded by kissy lips and tiny hearts, was waiting to be marked off. I fumbled in my purse for a pen. In order to get to it I managed to toss everything from lip gloss to receipts all over the floor. At any second I expected the hostess to walk over with a grim frown. Finally, I found the pen at the very bottom and I drew a careful line through the most important item on my list—Kiss Max.

"I can cross this off!" I grinned.

Max laughed as he watched me attack the paper with the pen. "It was an honor to be on the list."

I didn't mention that he'd always been on the list. I thought I'd fill him in on that later. I remembered adding the item again, and thinking that it was just a fool's dream.

Now it was my reality. It was done. It was my greatest accomplishment. Even as I marked it off, I still had a hard time believing it. I tucked the list back into my now empty purse and looked back at Max.

"It's not too late." I took his hand again. "It's exactly the right time."

I looked into his eyes. I saw our future unfolding. I didn't see a certain place or a certain timeline. Instead, I saw his hand remaining in mine.

A smattering of applause alerted me to the fact that several diners had been listening in. Normally I would have been mortified to have so much attention focused on me. But with Max's eyes locked to mine, I didn't even notice.

"I love you, Sammy."

"I love you too, Max."

We'd said those words to one another so many times, but this was the first time that we were honest about what they really meant.

Every single thought I'd ever had about kissing Max flooded my mind. I didn't wait for him to kiss me again.

Instead, my body filled with sparks as my lips approached his.

I expected him to pull away, I expected the restaurant to explode, I expected the ceiling to cave in on top of us. What I didn't expect was the tantalizing silk of his lips welcoming mine. Even in my wildest dreams, kissing Max had seemed impossible. But there in the restaurant where I'd been close to shedding tears over Blue's absence, I found my true love—my one and only love that had been by my side through thick and thin. My true love who was also my best friend.

My world spun, my body felt as if it was alive for the very first time. It was so much more than I'd imagined it would be. I was weak-kneed and out of breath, but I didn't want the kiss to ever stop.

Just when I thought it couldn't get any better, he slid his arms around my waist and drew my body close against his.

For the first time ever in my life, I felt as if I was exactly where I was meant to be.

A NOTE FROM THE AUTHOR

Fictional character, Samantha Bradford and the Single Wide Female books are written for every woman out there who has struggled with their weight, self-esteem and any number of issues that we all face as we work to become the best versions of ourselves that we can be.

These books are meant to be light-hearted and fun, with the hope that they will also inspire you to make your own "bucket list" of sorts—and to REALLY live your life to the fullest, loving yourself completely as you do so.

Lillianna loves to hear from her readers and can be contacted via her website where you can also download a complimentary book.

LilliannaBlake.com

ALL TITLES BY LILLIANNA BLAKE

http://Amazon.com/author/lilliannablake
*Check the author page for current list of titles

Single Wide Female in Love
#1 The Date
#2 The Girlfriend
#3 The Fiancée
#4 The Wife

Single Wide Female: The Bucket List
#1 Learn Pole Dancing
#2 Start a Blog
#3 Learn to Cook
#4 Create a Masterpiece
#5 Run a Marathon
#6 Go Skinny Dipping
#7 Start Online Dating
#8 Learn Yoga
#9 Be a Mentor
#10 Crash a Wedding
#11 Be a Movie Extra
#12 Join a Writing Group
#13 Enjoy a Spa Day
#14 Donate Blood
#15 Learn Poker
#16 Get a Tattoo

#17 Host a Dinner Party
#18 Publish a Book
#19 Walk Across Hot Coals
#20 Learn to Swim
#21 Learn to Meditate
#22 Quit My Job
#23 Learn to Salsa
#24 Fall in Love

Other Single Wide Female Titles
My Valentine's Day
St. Paddy's Day Disaster
A Bunny Tale

Becoming Zara
*how the B.I.G. Girls Club came to be

B.I.G. Girls Club
The Rockstar's Girlfriend
The Former Model

Visit the author website at LilliannaBlake.com to get on the notification list for new releases and to receive a complimentary book to learn what inspired Sammy to begin her bucket list.